T0272784

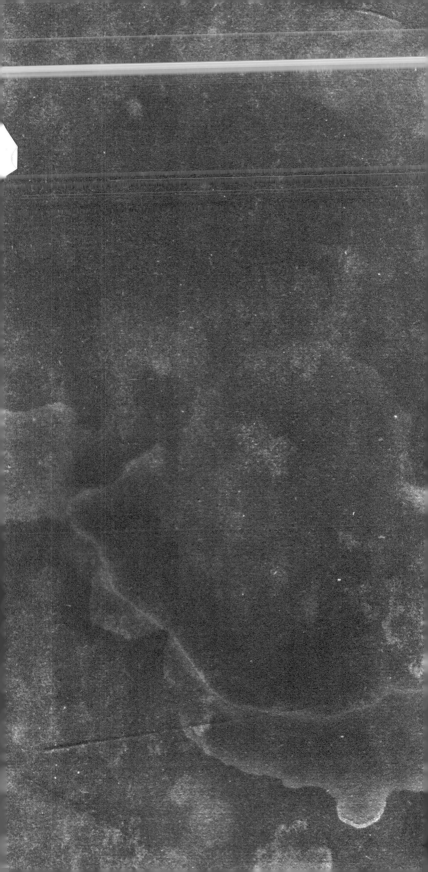

Blake Butler's *Scorch Atlas* is precisely that —a series of maps, or worlds, "tied so tight they couldn't crane their necks." Everything is either destroyed, rotting or festering—and not only the physical objects, but allegiances, hopes, covenants. Yet these worlds are not abstract exercises, he is speaking of life as it is, where there might be or may be, "glass over grave sites in display," and where we will be forced to make or where we have "made facemasks out of old newspapers." The sole glimmer of light comes in recollection, as in: "a bear the size of several men... There in the woods behind our house, when I was still a girl like you."

—**JESSE BALL**, author of *The Way Through Doors* and *Samedi the Deafness*

There's something so big about Blake Butler's writing. Big as men's heads. Each inhale of Blake's wheeze brings streamers of loose hair, the faces of lakes and oceans, whales washed up half-rotten. You can try putting on a facemask made out of old newspaper. You can breathe in smaller rhythms. But you won't be able to keep this man out once you've opened his book. Open it!

—**KEN SPARLING**, author of *Dad Says He Saw You at the Mall*

I am always looking for new writers like Blake Butler and rarely finding them, but *Scorch Atlas* is one of those truly original books that will make you remember where you were when you first read it. *Scorch Atlas* is relentless in its apocalyptic accumulation, the baroque language stunning in its brutality, and the result is a massive obliteration.

—**MICHAEL KIMBALL**, author of *Dear Everybody*

SCORCH ATLAS

A BELATED PRIMER

or

IN THE YEAR OF CYST & TREMOR

or

IN THE YEAR OF WORM & WILTING

or

OBLITERATIA

or

A BLOOM OF BLUE MOLD ALONG THE BACKBONE

or

A SLIP OF TONGUE IN THE YEAR OF YEAST

or

HIDE HIS EYES IN THE HIVE BLANKET

or

ILBLISSUM AKVISS NOEBLEERUM IGLITT PEEM

or

_____

or

NO WINDOW

or

SPOKE INTO THE SOFT SKIN OF THE MOTHER

or

WANT FOR WISH FOR NOWHERE

or

COMA OCEAN

or

GOODNIGHT.

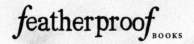

Copyright © 2009 by Blake Butler

All rights reserved. No part of this book may be reproduced in
any form or by any electronic or mechanical means, including
information storage and retrieval systems, without permission
in writing from the publisher, except in the case of short passages
quoted in reviews.

This is a work of fiction. All names, characters, places, and
incidents are the product of the author's imagination. Where the
names of actual celebrities or corporate entities appear, they are
used for fictional purposes and do not constitute assertions of fact.
Any resemblance to real events or persons, living or dead,
is coincidental.

Design: bleachedwhale.com

Published by
featherproof books
Chicago, Illinois
www.featherproof.com

First Edition

10 9 8 7 6 5 4 3 2

Library of Congress Control Number: 2008940499

ISBN: 0-9771992-8-2
ISBN 13: 978-0-9771992-8-0

Set in Quadraat

Printed in the United States of America

SCORCH ATLAS

BLAKE BUTLER

ACKNOWLEDGEMENTS

Gracious thanks to the editors of the journals in which these stories previously appeared in slightly altered forms, including:

'The Many Forms of Rain ___ Sent Upon Us' appeared in DIAGRAM's 2008 Innovative Fiction issue. Thanks to Ander Monson.

'The Disappeared' appeared in New Ohio Review (/nor). Thanks to John Bullock.

'Smoke House' appeared in Hobart. Thanks to Aaron Burch and Elizabeth Ellen.

'Gravel' appeared in Quick Fiction. Thanks to Adam and Jennifer Pieroni.

'Damage Claim Questionnaire' appeared in Lake Effect. Thanks to George Looney.

'Want for Wish for Nowhere' appeared in New York Tyrant. Thanks to GianCarlo DiTrapano.

'Television Milk' appeared in The Open Face Sandwich. Thanks to Alan Bajandas and Benjamin Solomon.

'The Gown from Mother's Stomach' appeared in Ninth Letter. Thanks to Jodee Stanley and Andrew Ervin.

'Seabed' appeared in Phoebe. Thanks to Ryan Call.

'Tour of the Drowned Neighborhood' appeared in Harpur Palate. Thanks to Barrett Bowlin.

'The Ruined Child' appeared in Barrelhouse. Thanks to Dave Housley, Matt Kirkpatrick, Mike Ingram, Joe Killiany, and Aaron Pease.

'Bath or Mud or Reclamation...' appeared in Avery Anthology and in Proximity as a mini-book. Thanks to Andrew Palmer, Steph Fiorelli, Adam Koehler, and Mairead Case.

'Water Damaged Photos of Our House Before I Left It' appeared in LIT. Thanks to Emily Taylor.

'Exponential' appeared in Willow Springs. Thanks to Sam Ligon.

Sections from 'Bloom Atlas' appeared in Ellipsis as 'Coma Ocean' and in Oranges & Sardines as 'Bloom Atlas.' Thanks to Carl Evans and Didi Menendez.

Caught by the rain far from shelter Macmann
    stopped and lay down, saying, The surface
    thus pressed against the ground will remain
    dry, whereas standing I would get uniformly
    wet all over, as if rain were a mere matter of
    drops per hour, like electricity.

Samuel Beckett, MALONE DIES

On the other hand, the sky on hot dustless days
    would leap with light, nails would wink in
    their boards, pails blaze like beacons, and
    the glass of the several stores would shout
    the sun at you, empty your head through
    your ears with whistling sunshine.

William Gass, THE TUNNEL

Contents

For anyone, most likely,
& in memory of Jeff

WATER

We watched our dirt go white, our crop fields blacken. Trees collapsed against the night. Insects masked our glass so thick we couldn't see. The husks of roach and possum filled the gutters. Every inch mucked with white film. All spring the sky sat stacked with haze so high and deep it seemed a wall, a lidless cover sealing in or sealing out. Those were stretched days, croaking. I don't know what about them broke. I don't know why the rain came down in endless veil. It streaked the cities, wiped the wires. It splashed the dust out from our cricked knees. It came a week straight, then another. The earth turned to mud and grass to slick. Minor homes sucked underground. Children were washed out in the sloshing. The streets and theme parks bubbled brown. Some long weeks it went on that way. The air began to mush downtown. We'd just taken up wearing knee boots and canoes to market when the soft water turned to ice. Our once parched apartments saddled under gleaming. The fat white bricks pounded the face of anything uncovered. It was the last week of July. Ice dented buildings, ruined car windshields, ripped limbs clean off of trees. I saw an old man clobbered in the street, his glasses shattered, his dentures flush with blood. The backyard stacked knee-deep around me. The drum woke tones deep in my ear. I couldn't sleep right. You never knew what might cave in. Frost killed the power, ruined the highways. Those who tried to drive were mostly mauled—run together in gagging slicks of solid liquid. Many neighborhoods froze enclosed. We spent uncounted ugly evenings with nowhere to look but at each other. When the TV finally came back, the news stations had such a backlog they began to list the names of the dead between commercials like the credits to some movie we wished we'd never seen.

THE
DISAPPEARED

The year they tested us for scoliosis, I took my shirt off in front of the whole gym. Even the cheerleaders saw my bruises. I'd been scratching in my sleep. Insects were coming in through cracks we couldn't find. There was something on the air. Noises from the attic. My skin was getting pale.

I was the first.

The several gym coaches, with their reflective scalps and high-cut shorts, crowded around me blowing whistles. They made me keep my shirt up over my head while they stood around and poked and pondered. Foul play was suspected. They sent directly for my father. They made him stand in the middle of the gym in front of everyone and shoot free-throws to prove he was a man. I didn't have to see to know. I heard the dribble and the inhale. He couldn't even hit the rim.

The police showed up and bent him over and led him by his face out to their car. You could hear him screaming in the lobby. He sounded like a woman.

For weeks after, I was well known. Even bookworms threw me up against the lockers, eyes gleaming. The teachers turned their backs. I swallowed several teeth. The sores kept getting worse. I was sent home and dosed with medication. I massaged cream into my wounds. I was not allowed to sleep alone. My uncle came to stay around me in the evenings. He sat in my mother's chair and watched TV. I told him not to sit there because no one did after Mother. Any day now Dad expected her return. He wanted to keep the smell of her worn inside the cracking leather until then. My uncle did not listen. He ordered porn on my father's cable bill. He turned the volume up and sat watching in his briefs while I stood there knowing I'd be blamed.

Those women had the mark of something brimming in them. Something ruined and old and endless, something gone.

By the third night, I couldn't stand. I slept in fever, soaked in vision. Skin cells showered from my soft scalp. My nostrils gushed with liquid. You could see patterns in my forehead—oblong clods of fat veins, knotted, dim. I crouped and cowed and cringed among the lack of moonlight. I felt my forehead coming off, the ooze of my blood becoming slower, full of glop. I felt surely soon I'd die and there'd be nothing left to dicker. I pulled a tapeworm from my ear.

My uncle sent for surgeons. They measured my neck and graphed my reason. Backed with their charts and smarts and tallies, they said there was nothing they could do. They retested my blood pressure and reflexes for good measure. They said say ah and stroked their chins. Then they went into the kitchen with my uncle and stood around drinking beer and cracking jokes.

The verdict on my father's incarceration was changed from abuse to vast neglect, coupled with involuntary impending manslaughter. His sentence was increased. They showed him on the news. On screen he did not look like the man I'd spent my life in rooms nearby. He didn't look like anyone I'd ever known.

The bugs continued to swarm my bedroom. Some had huge eyes. Some had teeth. From my sickbed I learned their patterns. They'd made tunnels through the floor. I watched them devour my winter coat. I watched them carry my drum kit off in pieces.

Another night I dreamed my mother. She had no hair. Her eyes were black. She came in through the window of my bedroom and hovered over. She kissed the crud out from my skin. Her cheeks filled with the throbbing. She filled me up with light.

The next morning my wounds had waned to splotches.

After a week, I was deemed well.

In the mirror my face looked smaller, somehow puckered, shrunken in. My eyes had changed from green to deep blue. The school required seven faxes of clearance before my readmission. Even then, no one came near me. I had to hand in my assignments laminated. I was reseated in far corners, my raised arm unacknowledged. Once I'd had the answers; now I spent the hours fingering the gum under my desk.

On weekends I went to visit Dad in prison. He was now serving twenty-five to life. They made him wear a plastic jumpsuit that enclosed his head to keep the felons' breath from spreading their ideas. Through the visor, my father's eyes were bloodshot, puffy. His teeth were turning brown. His small paunch from years of beer had flattened. He had a number on his arm. He refused to look at me directly. He either shook his head or nodded. This was my fault, I knew he thought. We spent our half-hour grunting, gumming, shrugged.

Each time before I left he asked one question, in sign language: HAS YOUR MOTHER FOUND HER WAY BACK YET?

Each time before I left he slipped me a ten and told me where to go.

At home we had a map of downtown that Dad kept on the kitchen table where we used to eat together. He'd marked with dated dots in fluorescent marker where he thought he'd seen her last. Mom was one of several who'd gone missing in recent weeks. Each night, between commercials, the news showed reams and reams of disappeared—pigtailed teens and Air Force pilots, stockbrokers, grandpas, unwed mothers. Hundreds had gone unaccounted. The missing ads covered milk cartons on every side. The government whispered *terrorism*. On the news they used our nation's other problems as distraction: the wilting trees; the mold-grown buildings, high-rise rooftops clung together; the color shift of oceans; the climaxed death rate of new babies.

The way the shores washed up with blood foam.

How at night you couldn't see the moon.

Before prison, Dad had sat at night with his cell phone on his knee on vibrate, waiting to feel the pulse shoot up his leg and hear her on the other end, alive. His skin would flex at any tremor. The phone rang through the night. The loan folks wanted back their money. Taxes. Electricity. They would not accept Visa or good will. Dad developed a tic and cursed with no control. He believed my mother's return in his heart. His list of sightings riddled the whole map. He thought he'd heard her once in the men's room at the movies. Once he'd seen her standing on the edge of a tobacco billboard, pointing down. He wanted me to keep tabs on all these places. As well, he wanted farther acres combed. Mom had been appearing in his sleep. She would not be hard to find if he truly loved her, he said she whispered. *You should already know by now.* On his skin, while in his cell bed, he made lists of the places where he should have looked: that spot in the ocean where he'd first kissed her; the small plot where they'd meant one day to be buried side by side; behind the moon where they joked they'd live forever; in places no one else could name. He wanted a full handwritten report of each location.

After school, before the sun dunked, I carried the map around the nearer streets in search. Sometimes, as my dad had, I felt mother's hair against my neck. I smelled her sweet sweat somehow pervading even in the heady rush of highway fumes. I heard her whistle no clear tune, the way she had with me inside her and when I was small enough to carry. I used the hours between school's end and draining light. I trolled the grocery, hiked the turnpike, stalked the dressing rooms of several local department stores. I felt that if I focused my effort to the right degree I could bring an end to all this sinking. I'd find her somewhere, lost and listless, lead her home, reteach her name. Newly aligned, she'd argue dad's innocence in court to vast amends, and then there'd be the three of us forever, fixed in the only home we'd ever known.

I did not find her at the creek bed where she'd taught me how to swim via immersion.

I spent several hopeful evenings outside the dry cleaners where she'd always taken all our clothes.

There were always small pools of buzzed air where I could feel her just behind me, or inside.

My uncle did not go home. He'd taken over my parents' bed and wore Dad's clothing. Through the night he snored so loud you could hear it throughout the house. You could hear as well the insects crawling: their tiny wings and writhing sensors. You could hear the wreathes of spore and fungus. The slither in the ground. It was all over, not just my house. Neighborhood trees hung thick with buzz. House roofs collapsed under heavy weight. Everyone had knives. They ran photo essays in the independent papers. The list of disappeared grew to include news anchors, journalists, and liberal pundits. I stayed awake and kept my hair combed. I tried not to walk in sludge.

I received an email from my father: SHE SAYS THERE'S NOT MUCH TIME.

I committed to further hours. I stayed up at night and blended in. I looked in smaller places: through the sidewalk; in the glare of stoplights; in the mouths of tagless dogs. I avoided major roads for the police. Out-of-town travel had been restricted. They mentioned our best interests. They said recovery begins at home. I marched through the forest with a flashlight, not quite laughing, being careful not to die. Trees fell at random in the black air. Anthills smothered whole backyards. It hadn't rained in half a year. You might start a mile-wide fire with one mislaid cigarette. The corporate news channel spent their hours showing pictures of dolphin babies and furry kittens cuddling in the breeze.

Meanwhile, at school, other people started getting sick. First, several players on the JV wrestling team shared a stage of ringworm—

bright white mold growths on their muscles. The reigning captain collapsed in the hot lunch line. They had to cancel future matches. The infestation was blamed on high heat and tight quarters. Days later, Jenny Rise, the head cheerleader, grew a massive boil on the left side of her head. It swelled the skin around her eyelids until she couldn't see. She went to the hospital not for the boil itself, but for how she'd tried to stab it out.

The seething moved in small creation through the cramped halls of our school. Popular kids got it. Kids with glasses. Kids in special ed. Teachers called out absent, then their subs did. Sometimes we were left in rooms unmanned for hours. There were so many missing they quit sending people home. Fast rashes rushed from collars. Guys showed up with their eyes puckered in glop. My lab partner, Maria Sanchez, grew a strange mustache. They had to sweep the hallways several times a day.

Instead of our usual assignments, we read manuals on how to better keep our bodies clean. Diagrams were posted in our lockers. Baskets of dental floss and disinfectant were placed in nurse's office with the condoms. No one really laughed.

Then, one day during my math class, men in military gear barged in. They had batons and air masks with complex reflectors. They made us stand in line with our hands against the wall. We spread and coughed while they roughed us over. They pulled hair samples and drew blood. From certain people they took skin grafts. The screaming filled the halls. They confiscated our cell phones and our book bags. Our class fish, Tommy, was deposed. The walls were doused with yellow powder. Several people fainted or threw up. They put black bags over the windows. The school's exit doors were sealed with putty. A voice that was not the cafeteria lady's came over the loudspeaker and said what was being served. We'd eaten lunch already. We sat at our desks and said the pledge. We sat at our desks with no one looking at each other. The sub for our sub was reprimanded for attempting exit. They laid her flat out on the ground.

We were contained this way without explanation. Because of the window bags, we couldn't tell how many days. There was a lot of time and no way to pass it. We were not allowed to talk or use the restroom. We were given crossword puzzles and origami. The PA played Bach and Brahms over the rumble overhead. When the lunchroom ran out of leftovers, we were fed through tubes lowered from the ceiling.

After the first rash of fistfights and paranoia spasms, they locked our wrists with plastic. They turned the a/c heat to high. The veins began to stand out on people's heads. Their skin went red and dented, then bright purple. Their hair fell out. Their teeth and nails grew green and yellow. Their swollen limbs bejeweled with sores. Cysts blew big in new balloons.

I felt fine. I felt an aura, my mother's breath encircling my head.

The costumed men carried the expired elsewhere. Those who weren't sick were crazed. I watched a girl bang her face in on a blackboard. I watched a boy stick out his eyes. The rest of us sat with our hands flat on the desktops, not sure which way to turn.

Soon the power was extinguished. False neon panels were employed. Peals of static began to interrupt the PA's symphonies. A sudden voice squawked through with contraband report. *Look what we've done. Can you imagine? Half the nation under quarantine. The buildings crumpled. The oceans aboil. The President's committed suicide. And now, just a bit too late, we're getting rain.* The men burst in and shot the speaker with a machine gun. They said to assume the duck and cover. One spotty redhead whose glasses had been confiscated refused to get down. She walked around in small circles reaching from desk to desk to guide her way. The men zapped her in the neck with a large prong. She ran straight into a wall. She fell on the floor and bumped her forehead, and it spilled open on the white tile. None of the men would let me help them help her. They carried her out and wrapped our heads in plastic and went into the hall and shut the door. I heard the tumblers clicking in the lock. I saw the hall fill thick with smoke. There were sirens, screech and screaming. Something scraping on the roof. It wasn't long yet until other. I didn't try to think of what. Small Susie Wang huddled beside me, praying. She spoke in hyperventilated mumble. She put her hands over her mouth.

I sat on the floor in the neon light with stomach rumbling and sounds of flame and stink of rot. I saw things moving toward me and then gone. I couldn't remember where or why I was. I couldn't find my name writ on my tongue or brain-embedded. I felt a burning in my chest. I fumbled in my pockets for my father's map. I stared and rubbed the paper between my fingers. I read the sightings' dot's dates with my wormed eyes, connecting them in order. There was the first point where my father felt sure he'd seen mother digging in the neighbor's yard across the street. And the second, in the field of power wires where Dad swore he saw her running at full speed.

I connected dots until the first fifteen together formed a nostril. Dots 16 through 34 became an eye.

Together the whole map made a perfect picture of my mother's missing head.

If I stared into the face, then, and focused on one clear section and let my brain go loose, I saw my mother's eyes come open. I saw her mouth begin to move. Her voice echoed deep inside me, clear and brimming, bright, alive.

She said, "Don't worry, son. I'm fat and happy. They have cake here. My hair is clean."

She said, "The earth is slurred and I am sorry."

She said, "You are OK. I have your mind."

Her eyes seemed to swim around me. I felt her fingers in my hair. She whispered things she'd never mentioned. She nuzzled gleamings in my brain. As in: the day I'd drawn her flowers because all the fields were dying. As in: the downed bird we'd cleaned and given a name. Some of our years were wall to wall with wonder, she reminded me. In spite of any absence, we had that.

I thought of my father, alone and elsewhere, his head cradled in his hands. I thought of the day he'd punched a hole straight through the kitchen wall, thinking she'd be tucked away inside. All those places he'd looked and never found her. Inside their mattress. In stained-glass windows. How he'd scoured the carpet for her stray hair and strung them all together with a ribbon; how he'd slept with that one lock swathed across his nostrils, hugging a pillow fitted with her nightshirt. How he'd dug up the backyard, stripped and sweating. How he'd played her favorite album on repeat and loud, a lure. How when we took up the carpet in my bedroom to find her, under the carpet there was wood. Under the wood there was cracked concrete. Under the concrete there was dirt. Under the dirt there was a cavity of water. I swam down into the water with my nose clenched and lungs burning in my chest but I could not find the bottom and I couldn't see a thing.

DUST

Dry flakes of charcoal came big as men's heads, slather from some great fire overhead. The ash rained black into the evening, clung against the mud as some new second skin. Each inch sat spackled, crusted over. Each inhale brought a mouthful. The streets intoned with choral wheeze and incensed hiccup. We made facemasks out of old newspapers— the current editions no longer came. The mail service had gone under—one minor blessing: I stopped receiving bills. The finer dust came down in curling spigots. The sick began to bundle, hung at home. Count emphysema. Count belabored lungs. As well: asthma, croup and coughing. The air so thick we called it paste. Strung among the gusts came reams of loose hair. Blonde or black streamers stole from sore heads. Cells clogged the chimney, laced the evening. Though the TV went out again in interference, radioed men spoke the wreckage even in our sleep: whole apartment buildings ransacked in skin flakes; baseball stadiums filled to the brim; the faces of lakes and oceans so thick that you could walk forever. The plumes of powder flew over our yards. It beat against our windows, making bass. I learned to breathe in smaller rhythms. The incubated heat swelled so high outside you'd sweat forever, then more dust. Eyes encrusted. Nostrils clogged. One night, finally, the roof over my living room succumbed to all the weight. Somewhere in there, under all that dander, I often would regret I had not been.

SMOKE
HOUSE

Nights at home now the house sat wordless, so still the mother could not sleep. The bed cramped small and dirty; the air above her suffocating. The mother in her nightgown, tight, worn ratty where she rubbed her fingers in worry circles. She got up and left her husband crimped with his back toward her on the mattress and went downstairs. She went through the kitchen stuffed full of flowers, long rotten, stinking. She went into the son's room where plastic sheeting covered the holes the fire had burned. The pinned laminate tacked in short sheets over the studs to keep the outside out or inside in. There was no wind. Outside, the earth lay parched and cracking. The trees enfolding over black lawns. The sky only ever one dumb color.

The mother stood in the exact center of the son's room, or what remained of it. The room could be divided into halves: here, from the window to the far corner, where the walls were smudged and plaster dappled and the scorching sat upon the air; and here, past the window to the closet, where much of her son's stuff sat untouched: the shirt he'd slept in every night since he was ten; the blanket the mother had sewn for him while he was still inside her; the trombone he begged for and never played. Each item encoded with his touch.

Before the son had moved into it, before they'd had a son at all, the burned room had been the master. In that room they'd made the child. He'd been a glimmer in their flat lives. A thing mistaken in the mother as a tumor until the infant sledded out, unbreathing. They'd nearly given up, and now this light. They'd had another child not long after: a thin-skinned daughter, soft of bone, another error no less loved. The house could not contain them. They'd built a new room on the upstairs. The son had taken the old master, where fifteen years later, the air would burn.

They could have let him have the newer room instead.

They could have built several rooms—halls and halls and on forever.

The son could still be with them now.

So many nights the son had come through the house sleepwalking, knocking pictures off the walls. Sometimes he'd stood before her naked, cut with muscle; the look in his eyes blasted, vacant, as she guided him back to bed.

The mother's back ached. Her throat was dry as outside, wracked with unseen lesions, rheum. She lay down on the blackened carpet, the stink of old smoke hung around her head. She writhed and rubbed against it, smearing soot along her neck, her gown, her hair.

■

Upstairs the father watched the ceiling. He'd faked deep slumber through his wife's long sobs. Another night. He knew he should touch her but he didn't. He could not find a way to spread the intent through his body. He heard her fumble in the ill light. He kept his body fully flexed—mocked in the language of unconscious. She closed the door softly behind her. She'd always been considerate. She'd always kept measured ways around him, despite his caw, despite his bitching. He'd never figured out exactly how to express certain things—just saying them seemed too cheap.

Above the bed there was a skylight which when the room was designed had seemed ideal. Endless slumber under moon glow. An eye into the night. Instead the portal proved offensive—the sun's angle woke him every morning. It let unwanted modes into his sleeping. He dreamt of black stars exploding in his cheeks; strange figures crawling through his veins behind his forehead; shit spurting from his pores. He'd covered the opening with foam rubber, causing the room to glow at a slight mute. The bed absorbed an aura. At dusk, the sheen of glass would reflect his head back at his eyes. The eyes were always open when he saw them, waiting until he nodded off. *Always there. Another self.* Finally one night while sleeping he'd stood with his feet sinking in the mattress and banged the glass out with his fists until he bled. Now they slept in open air.

In bed alone, the father thought of when he'd tried to teach his son to shave. How the child refused to let him help. How the son had cut his cheek so deep it spurted on the mirror. His son there screaming, face meat covered in white foam, blood sluicing and mixing with the lather; son screaming at the father to go away. That bathroom, where years before, when it was just them, he'd held the mother in the mirror, making four.

The father shuddered on the mattress, wanting a way to lie that would keep his back and neck from crimping, a configuration in which he could finally click into deep sleep, deep enough to maybe never wake, while in the ruined room below him, his wife wallowed in rhythm, just the same.

■

The house had caught on fire seven times in seven months. Each time it had ignited in a new location, if contained:

(1) the downstairs foyer, where the family's portrait hung, a value-bought multi-pack, the same shot the Dad kept crumpled in his wallet, and the daughter scratched with marker, hid in a drawer;

(2) inside a kitchen cabinet (the kiddie plates had stunk for weeks, their neon gobs still globbed in puddles, the countertop all warped);

(3) in the backyard, where several pets were buried, as were other things of which the family did not know;

(4) along the rooftop and through the attic, ruining several unmatched heirlooms and their plastic Christmas tree, made black;

(5) in the washroom dryer, ruining all the clothes the father ever really wore;

(6) in the guestroom closet, empty;

(7) around the son.

Each time the house had glowed in brief fury under the canopy of night. Always under star strum. Always while they slept.

The parents wanted elsewhere. They could not afford to move before they sold the house. They could not sell the house. Each potential buyer who came for viewing left with a strange look on their face. The insurance company sent inspectors who could not determine a clear cause of the frequent combustion. Other buildings had caught fire in the local area from the dry weather, but none so many times as theirs. The insurance company had placed their file under review. Some people used the term *bad fortune*. The mother's mother said into the phone, *Y'all aren't living right*.

The mother could not understand what had changed. They'd lived in the house for twenty years. They'd never once had a problem, but now the roof creaked, and the fires. The mirrors came loose in the bathrooms and fell forward, smashed to bits. The carpet curled up around the corners exposing the smooth green speckled foam beneath. There were often sounds of creaking, louder and more violent than the normal settling of a house: sounds of bones in fingers breaking, something crumpled promptly growing old.

The mother often felt people standing in the caves behind her. Once, in the sun room, she'd seen her father. Sometimes she heard him in the air vents, in the shower, in the whir of the garage door's rise. The main thing she could remember of him after all these years was how his teeth would fall out then grow right back in, one set after another. *What made her remember that?* That hadn't happened. No, she knew he'd kept the sheddings in a small box in his dresser. When he was out, she'd go and look at them all corralled there, a field of enamel, yellowed, sharp.

For years she dreamed of those teeth appearing in her own gums.

For years those teeth lived in her brain.

■

Some nights the father would stand outside the house and still feel its walls surrounding. From enough distance he could pinch the brick between his thumb and finger, hide the light. When he did, his sternum shook, sometimes for days.

■

The son was underground. The seventh fire seemed to have begun inside his mattress. It had engulfed him in his sleep and cracked his teenage skin. They'd assumed at first that he was smoking, but they found no butt, no match, no lighter. The son had been good at school. He'd been respected. He had a girlfriend many others would've liked to touch. He was on the swim team and wrote A papers and he won when he played chess. His flesh had partly melded with the mattress. His burning browned the wall and let the moon in. It made a pattern on the ceiling. The ground he was in now was rife with larvae. The mud was bright red and cold and endless. There were sounds that moved through the earth that people above it could not hear.

Before his exit, the son had taken a picture of himself every morning upon waking. He kept the pictures in sequential order, hidden, on the hard drive of his computer. He wanted to one day be able to look at the files and observe his catalog of aging. He'd never told anyone about this practice. The pictures were still there, saved, somehow preserved amidst the heat.

If the mother had known about the pictures, she would have kept them hidden, *for herself*. She would have noticed how, in the last several months of photographing, something began to creep into the film. How in the air around her son's head grew a small buzzing, aligned in the photo as a slight blur. How over the last weeks before the son's death the photos had begun to grow so ruined you could not see most of his face—how the film grew embedded with fields of bright botched color: shades of pink and brown and orange and green—and somewhere inside that, strange—his eyes.

■

The daughter had begun to convince herself that this was all her fault. First, she'd made the house swell, though not enough. She'd recognized a short strain of curse in her surroundings that continued to grow worse as she got older. Everyone she liked at school got sick or moved away. When she touched the television screen it shocked her. When she picked out a loaf of bread at the grocery, she always found a spore of mold inside. She always bumped her head against things. She was always itching. She couldn't sleep.

But it was much worse than all of that. She'd hurt a man once, without intention. He was crossing the street and she looked at him and he smiled. A car hit him from the side. He fell on the gravel and spurted blood. He looked her directly in the eyes. She still had the dress she'd worn that day, with the spattering across it. She'd buried it in the transom of her closet, under the old dolls and books and raincoats.

Another time she'd been staring at an airplane and it fell right out of the sky. Just like that. She didn't know what was wrong with her but there was something. She could feel a bump deep inside her forehead. A murmur in her hair. She knew the house kept burning because she was in it. Because it wanted her made gone.

And now, because she hadn't listened, her brother turned to char. Who knew what else she had made happen. Who knew what else she would destroy. She tried to explain these things but no one would listen. She felt older than she looked.

In the night, with her parents elsewhere, she sat in her closet with the old dress and pressed the man's brown stains against her face.

■

- I know you're awake.
- I'm not awake.
- You're talking.
- That's someone other talking for me.
- How cute. How clever.
- (sounds of snoring)
- Quite. Well, you enjoy. (moves past the bed into the bathroom; sound of rummaging through drawers)
- What's going on?
- I'm looking for my lighter. You'll forget me in a minute.
- Your lighter? You bought cigarettes?
- I didn't.
- Give me one.
- I said I didn't buy any cigarettes.
- Then why the lighter?
- (long pause) It was Dad's. I want to hold it. I need something. You're not you.
- You expect me to believe that? Why not just say it? I'm not what?
- (slick metal sounds of an old hinge clicking) Here it is. (closes the drawer; moves through the bedroom back to the door again; glares at the bed) Night.
- What's the black crap you've got all over you? ___?
- (door opens and door closes)
- (does not say goodnight)

■

Her left hand's thumb flicked the metal wheel that ground and spit a flame into the nothing—the yellow neon tremble of fluid burning—the shimmer of incendiary air suffused with fume. The mother's hand trembled just slightly. She'd always had small fingers, good for sewing, good for cleaning out one's ears.

The metal lighter really had belonged once to her father; in fact, he'd meant to take it with him. Eight years old, there, at the coffin, she'd slipped her hand into the gone man's pockets, not understanding, maybe after money, maybe scent, the teeth, some *something to remember.* The lifeless head's lips grinned—he could feel her rummaging around him, tickled. She'd found the lighter there over his heart, soft-brushed and gleaming, full of fluid. No one was looking. She'd hid it in her best dress, cold against her skin. The lighter was always cold.

Sometimes now, thirty years later, she still felt the soft slur of something strumming when she smoked, as if it were her father's smoky dead breath that ballooned behind her cheeks. She couldn't even remember how he died.

The mother held the lighted lighter in her son's room again, inhaling the scum of the blackened walls with the tobacco smoke, the outlined spot on the floor where once there'd been a bed, where once on that bed she'd sat reading the child stories till he was old enough to read them back, cut from her voice.

The mother took the lighter to the window. She went to press her face against the glass, to butt it hard and feel the impact, then remembered how the glass was no longer there—how it'd been cracked by heat or kicked out by men in flame-retardant coats to let water through. She felt her head go on out into the evening, into the cupped light overhead. There was no moon or streetlamps glowing, no trees still lit up in tall torches as when the backyard had caught ignition. Just long black and stagnant fields of air, the wind settled, calm again, under glass.

The mother felt the lighter's metal getting warm. She kept her fingers close against it. She sniffed the air inside the room that'd burned her son. She leaned against the window's empty frame, the air so arid she could smell its quiver, a flux between here and there, surrounded.

■

That night, instead of burning, the first rain in many months and miles poured on the night. The water poured as something above had come undone, a full urn busted and expulsing. It graced the nearby empty creek beds and the dead lawns, the ratty sprats of trampled fields. It pocked the long face of so much dried mud, in which so many other things were buried. It slicked the roofs from which now many had jumped, or dreamt it, or wished they really would.

The rain did not announce itself. It came.

It came through the open skylight window and drummed the father, who hadn't slept yet but still had dreams: of a warm house he'd envisioned somewhere. He let the water spot his forehead, soak the pillow. He lay blinkless and unmoving while it glossed his cracked lips and tongue. He drank. He drank—and then he sat up, sat on the mattress and thought of words he'd never thought before.

The water found the daughter in her bedroom, inside the swelling house, the old cells bumping, crimping the indenture of the closet where piled neck-deep with old clothes she'd begun to rise off of the floor.

The water filtered through the dead son. It soaked through the warped lid of his casket—through his desiccating skin into his bones and through his dry veins. It filled the soil with mumble as from insects, as the stirrings of the house.

It drenched the mother in her nightgown, through the already flooded gutters in the street. From nowhere and everywhere at once. It washed the soot clean from the mother's cheeks. It slapped her hair and drenched the ashes. It ran in forked ways down her scratched skin—speaking—*that this rain is some beginning*—*that this rain might never cease.*

GRAVEL

The day the sky rained gravel I watched it drum my father's car.
A Corvette he'd spent years rebuilding. He liked to watch his face
gleam in the hood. He kissed the key before ignition. He read the
owner's manual aloud. When he lost the strength to stand he left
the car uncovered in the street. Each morning I took a Polaroïd and
we tacked it to his headboard—a panorama of slow ruin. After four
years, the car's wear matched the sallow skin of his sick head. He
had me bring the smell of the old leather to him in plastic bags. He'd
always said something was coming. He'd always said the world had
no idea. Imagine him in bed on that gray day. Imagine him wishing he
could drive at 80 through the downpour down to where the tide had
begun to expel foam. Where the whales washed up half-rotten, their
huge, soft heads brained by the hailing stone. The gravel piled up on
the front lawn, covering the pets we'd already buried, one each year.
I'd never been good at keeping things alive. On my own headboard
I cut notches. The Corvette's paint came off in yellow divots, my
father's hair loose on the pillow. His teeth were weak. He sucked a
bottle. Soon the car's roof caved. Imagine my father's baby chipped
to bits. Shit falling out of orbit. The scream of others down the street.
Imagine the soapy loam covering the beach sand where for years he
and I had fried. Where with our skin still raw and itching we'd fit our
church clothes over our swimsuits. If I'd listened, in those soft days,
I would have taken other pictures to show my children (the children
I'll never have). I'd flip through the photo album backwards and
watch my father's head grow full again—and me smaller, brighter
eyed, head shook clean of later days. Imagine the endless pummel
of our sore home. The sound of the bigger buildings bowing. How
my father insisted I help him to the kitchen so he could see out to
the street—where the car sat six feet under, smothered. The stink
of the ocean through the glass. Imagine us there together. Imagine
the billow of his eye. Imagine the way the hail slowed to let the sun
through before it really started coming down.

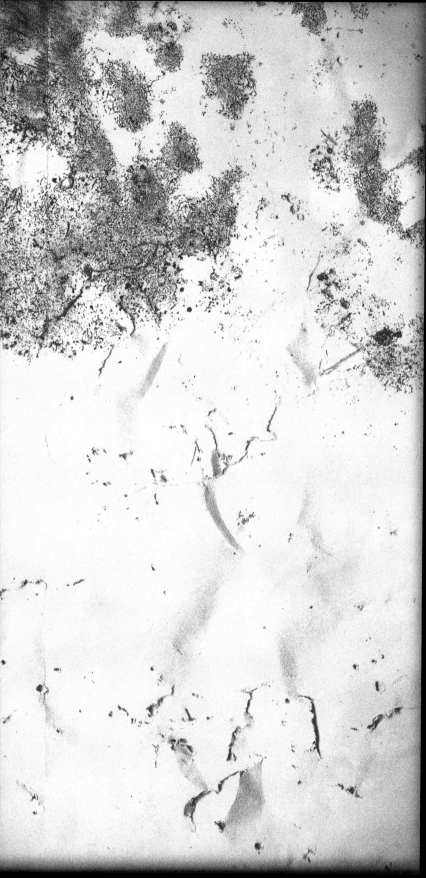

DAMAGE CLAIM
QUESTIONNAIRE

WHERE WERE YOU THAT EVENING?

—My hair was six feet long. I sat wrapped inside it in the kitchen—a gown of deceased cells. Outside the kids from next door beat the house and brayed. Days before, I'd watched their father swan dive from their roof onto the lawn. Their father, the electrician, with the tumor on his cheek. Such grace as he held his hands together and aimed straight for the dirt—he knew already what was coming—he'd sensed the ruining air. Now his boys needed me for feeding; to comb the gnats out of their lashes. But I was so done in already. Even then I lacked most all.

WHAT WAS HUMMING?

—I still taste the songs I gave my baby. You could read his features through my casing. I coughed rheumy refrain between my soft teeth, my voice cragged as my dad's had through years consuming Red Man and Listerine. He never spat. My eyes bugged with the brush of tongue to palate as I struggled with each note. To sing above the sound of outside. The insects make the most. You think you'd learn to overlook the flutter. The curdle of wallpaper. Ever smash a roach bug with a dictionary? Sometimes you hear them scream. A lady screams much different. I grew up in the South. My headache bred from years of scummy water and inhaled dust. The years of home a house holds aren't in wood so much as air.

HOW LONG HAVE YOU OWNED YOUR HOME?

—Rick and I ate breakfast every morning for seven years without a blank. He made shrimp and grits with bacon and honey crumpets with black jam. They say O.J. is full of larvae but we drank it in great gulps. Sometimes still I feel them blooming in my throat. Rick would read out loud from the Bible with his mouth full of the grease. He used plastic forks for fear of electrocution. His gold-capped teeth would buzz. At night we slept back to back, kissing vertebrae, interlocked. You couldn't convince me we'd but spent one life together. You couldn't say he didn't love our son, though he left while I was still engorged—a minor heartbeat matching mine; and the drumbeat of my abdomen as our small boy kicked and kicked, in want to puncture his poor mother's waistline and emerge in time to watch the squall.

LIST THE ESTIMATED VALUE OF DAMAGE.

—Twin storm fences, wrecked. Top grade sod, uplifted. The soil turned pink and sponged. Roof puckered, pocked with bird shit. Concrete driveway cracked and scattered. We had a stone angel in the courtyard that'd already lost its arm. I saw that angel fly—lifted off in clean ascension to somewhere we would not see. Swimming pool infested. Lawnmower rusted. Paint on the Chevy hailed obscene. Hardwoods in the den and guest room warped, already rotting. Plumbing pushed up through the floor. Rocking chair run off with. Mildewed carpet. Roach parade. Can we claim instances of soft disease? I'll show you rickets, nausea, itching. I reckon we can dicker. I'll sign my name if I can recall the way it went.

HAVE YOU UNDERTAKEN METHODS TO PROTECT AGAINST FURTHER LOSS?

—I often think of pastry. My joints creak when it drizzles. The windows have been painted over. I'd never kiss another man. The baby calm inside me, his kick stilled off to numb. Some evenings I walk the rows of houses and put my face against their glass, peering past the insides where some cold hours after dinner they'd sit around and stare. I found wax flowers in several kitchens and tied them through my hair. My brain is soggy. Mostly I just shed.

CAN YOU STILL SMELL THE NIGHT?

—Many times the sky comes open. The flap of heaven fixed there, fanning. Nothing. I'd sooner prefer sit here in the tub and run the water and watch it spill onto the tile. Thump my belly. Whisper to him. Wait for strumming. Something new. Feel my skin go older quicker, the wet running up my old folds. The smell of mold drawn in the water. Toothpaste dinner. Constant wake. My hair draped on my shoulders wet and shades darker, like a scarf. Sopping and sagging I trundle under, wondering how long it would take to prune my tired face unrecognizable.

A JEW, A SHRINK AND AN ASSHOLE ALL WALK INTO A BAR...

—Thanks for your well wishing. I understand the want for jokes. My throat is ripping, clogged and cracked now. My back creaks when I think. I pray into my dirt most evenings for the urge to snicker again, green. You should see what's become of our peach trees. The bloat. The blackened axis. The bow and bending of our city buildings. Slow roll of corrosion. If I had the nerve I'd build a guitar. I'd string it with my hair, white at age twenty. I'd play in rhythm with my stomach—the new roar that's replaced our baby's bump. The boggy burp's best bass. Oh, what songs we'd make together, me and my doppelganger, cheek to cheek.

COULD YOU BE DOING SOMETHING MORE?

—I spend my evenings these days in the kitchen. I knit new clothes for our child. I learned to knit after the death of cable TV. I use colored wires ripped from dumb machines. I would have made him bonnets. A cape. A canopy above his crib. My lips would tickle the stubble on his under-neck once he was old. *Tell your mother where you've been.* Now that he's quiet and the skies have settled shortly, I hold my grieving in the folds of my elbows, neck and knees. The way time robs in futures pissed. Sleep-rooms in pools up to your crown. I'd have liked to think me kinder, but the neighbor—I hear his kids beg and think: *coffin nails.* Sometimes I know they're not even there. That their pounding is only more of my dumb pulse.

HOW WILL YOU REMEMBER?

—In my loose teeth. In my knocking knees. With the stripe of morning across the yard; where the worms rise, where the earth spits up its dinner. This house grows older with me every night. How I'll remember? In the burning. In the cloud rattle. Each time the roof thuds above me. Each time I wet my face in squirm. And there's always all this paper—our receipts, shorthand and thank yous, birthday rhymes composed by strangers; notes and trash and mail unopened; photographs, if water-warped. Sometimes I recite my life aloud for hours. Sometimes I just don't have the heart.

GLASS

The glass came first in early morning. I watched through the only safe storm window. The sound of sky come ripping—some sour music box, cranked to crack. The panes shattered on impact, each giving off a second spray. We watched the dead yards, already buried, now held under new refracted light. Glass over grave sites in display. Glass slit through awnings, billboard faces. The facemasks became more dire in the scatter, each inhale suspect, lined with slice. Glass specks embedded in our eyelids—count the new ranks of the blind. The glass came in many colors: some pure translucent, however tarnished; green and brown burst bottles; backed with silver as in mirrors; blue from Depression-era heirlooms; stained from the awe-stuck eaves of churches. The shriek of glass on glass peeled my skin. The screech of all things scorched around me. The brassy, tinkled detonation. Shards of wronged birds. Real birds impaled and writhing. Even the sun had hid its eye. We were several layers under now. We could not think of other times. We called truce and splayed our fingers. The sky would not forgive.

WANT FOR
WISH FOR
NOWHERE

My first child splurged inside me. He ate what I ate—ate it all. There never was enough: my milk, my eggs and honey, my hunks of ham and strange things craved. I picked gnats out of the carpet; chewed through the shower curtain; swallowed blood. *Baby hungry. Baby want.* His teeth nicked in my linings. He tore my inner-skin, his nails already long and gleaming in the manner of what I used to shave my pits.

I would not contain him long.

Soon my belly was my body. All my weight belonged to him. I stooped through the apartment, cords in my back clenched. I still lived alone in those days. The man who'd helped me make the baby had left to find his way into the television. Specks of skins of selves he'd been in other years still lay around me on the air; and, as such, I'd breathe him in. I pulled his long hair from the sink pipes. I swelled with child until I could not stand. Until I could not remember where I was or where I'd been, whenever. I'd find myself on the phone with no one. I'd find my fingers caked with grease and the window open, half-hung on the sill to jump.

To keep my wits about me, I whispered to the child. Certain words called walls of color though my vision: *where* washed my day with yellow, *ouch* tickled green, *tomorrow* pink. Other terms caused lengthy tones to nestle in my ear, tympanic. Sometimes the ceiling would be caving. Other nights I couldn't see.

My hair began to fall out. My face stopped looking like my face.

Then one night I felt something open in me. Then one night I knew: a window. A threshold gunning in my stomach. I felt several things collide.

I crawled to the front door and out into the breezeway, where the air stung, where the porch lights had burnt away. The pods of moths still swarmed around them. You could see them strumming on the moon. The scummy husk of their glazed wing skin. The wooze. Trees had overgrown the stairs.

I cooed, my belly bulging, my hope composed in newborn bone.

I might have gone on alone forever.

I'm still not sure who took me in.

■

On the table, they cut me open. I observed from overhead. I watched them rip a seam straight up my middle. The curdle of my insides spread into the room—some kind of flesh-held flower. My eyes were open. My skin was white.

The doctors supplanted my softer parts with metal. They affixed me with a mask. If there was sound, I could not hear it over the fluorescence; the churn of something in me, bruised, innate. Small raw spots clung among the corners of my phantom vision. I felt a gauze around my head. I kept pulling at it, my short breath shaking. I swam over myself.

And from myself, from out of me, came my firstborn, came the boy.

There he was. The him. The seedling.

I watched him rise up from my gut.

I watched in silence, vibrating slightly.

I'd wanted so long for something somewhere.

I did not expect to be called back down.

■

The boy was very large. His skin was slick and bright and runny. The doctors strained to lift him out. There was squealing on the air.

Back in my body, I saw ultraviolet. The room's girders trembled. The gum.

The walls folded and unfolded. I could not taste my tongue.

The baby measured longer than a machete—his massive skull, ruined fruit. His chest and belly were splotched with something. His head of hair—blonde like Father's—grew over his ears across his cheeks. It'd spread over his eyelids. I could see him. He could not see me.

They took him somewhere else to clean him. I heard a whisper in my ear.

I watched, half-spinning, while they sewed me up, a long rosebud in my gut, matching the one I had inside me. I could still feel the gap from where the boy had been. I waited for him there inside my arms.

They did not bring him.

They did not bring him.

I screamed a sermon at the roof.

I screamed for him to appear before me. For what I needed. In the itch.

I suffered such a long stretch of expectation curdled in my yearning. The years and years of days unraveled. Everything at once seemed far away. Far and cold and small and wilting.

Please, I stuttered, scumming. *Please me.*

They hushed and shushed and there-there patted. They shoveled applesauce into my mouth. I spat the pap back at them out onto my bib, all dizzy. The lights went in and out around.

I continued: *Where's my baby? What's the number? Press him to me.*

The answers sprang back from within: *You are not ready. The time is never. He won't live.*

And overhead, the flicker: day, then night, day, night.

■

Some evenings later, I took the child home in a sack provided by the state. He could not yet be exposed to sunlight, considering the sky—scratched and black and bumpy. I hadn't seen a bird in weeks. The air was full and smelled of burning and in some winds, seemed to speak.

With the child, the state had sent a pamphlet of instructional directives. The list weighed twenty-seven pounds. I memorized the key points in my downtime, aloud and sing-song, a dream hymn—

- *There are holes in every home.*
- *Consider the effect of certain light in/around/against the child and/or its skin.*
- *If you become tired, someone is always awake somewhere. Rest well.*
- *Try to smile.*
- *Effective punishments of rash behavior in the infant may include: threat of hair loss, short confinement, gravel picnic, bad percussion, systematic slurring of education, heavy bath.*
- *Sometimes, to invoke power, pretend the child is not quite there.*
- *Sometimes put the child's eyes to your eyes.*

Despite whatever medication they'd injected, or what creams I might apply, the child's skin kept mostly muddled. His rind was thick and multicolored, prone to sore. He often oozed. He smelled of cabbage. He was in there, still, I knew. I had to peel his lids to see his pupils spinning—neon yellow, again like Father's. He seemed easy in his body. He came up to my waist. At six days old, he ate two-fisted from the fridge. I could not keep anything slick or sweet around. He ate the meat before I cooked it. He drank the soup straight out of cans. He'd burp and laugh with his whole body.

His genitals were shriveled and oddly colored.

His fingerprints were whorled.

On okay afternoons, we went walking through the forest that had choked the half-backyard. The trees were gnarled and beat and bare of leaves, save for in spots so high above us we couldn't see, in which case the blooms of mold became a canopy. There'd been a stream here somewhere once whose nightly murmurations sent me somewhat sleeping—but now it'd evaporated or sunk to mud. The yard as well was strewn with garbage. There were never any men. We ran neon tape behind us to mark the way. We walked into the fold. I showed him where I'd laughed once, and said what had been there then. The dirt often seemed to breathe.

At the wide-warped bow of land burnt by lightning, ripped wide-open, slick with mud, I told my huge son of the house we'd had there when I was his age, before the running, before the rape.

At the raze of black rock damming the river dry, I described the days I'd gone swimming with my brother—the water level just above our stomachs, the current ever-begging to take us down.

I did not tell him what I would have done differently, had I known then.

We glimpsed the charred valley where the sun rose sometimes
and the bulb of maggots over McDonald's
and the crisp crust of something unknown on the cold sand where I and his father had dug our dinner. I tried not to speak ill of that sore man, that absence. I tried not to let on my vehemence. I spoke in rhyme and benediction. I kept any anger hidden, scrunched to a tight pellet in my stomach, seamed with heat.

Mostly, through all my talking, the boy blinked and cawed and chewed his lip. Sometimes he'd respond in giggles, grunting, sinking his teeth into his bone. Whether he understood or not, it didn't matter—my words were seeping in. They'd spread his flesh and find a holster. He'd look back one day and understand.

I'd make this world somewhere to rest in. He'd remember.

We would not grow old alone.

■

As weeks got worse—the earth's plates snapping; the flies at the window cracking the glass; the stitch of rhythm in the incision of the earth sinking in itself—my boy continued to grow faster. I could not sew fast enough to clothe him. He would stretch a pair of pants in several days. In his large hands I saw the wrinkles of other ways that I had known.

Soon he was a man.

Already he was grown so large I couldn't fit him in my arms.

I called him different names for each occasion. He responded to them all.

It was cold in the apartment. The heater mostly did not work. We could see our breath in long shapes, crystallizing. The freeze air made him violent. He unstuffed the sofa and ruined my magazines. He took the heads off all his dolls.

Such a busy child. So eager. He didn't mean to bruise my face. He only wanted, like me, something he could hold a certain way.

In the evenings, once he'd grown worn out, the apartment again reduced to shambles, I put my hours towards attempting to teach him how to speak. He'd already proved a want for learning. He liked to watch my tapes of old TV. I'd spent hundreds cataloging my favorite programs back when the broadcasts were still on air: the answers and storylines of which I could not at all remember. The people in those pictures seemed very different from people now. Their eyes were slightly wider. Their skin offered a sheen.

My son could somehow see them through his barbed hair, which no matter how quickly I cut it from him, would grow back straight and further black.

In the newsreels I'd acquired, letting the VCR spool on through the night, I let my baby witness the swan dive of our destruction as arrayed in mini-clips—the anchors with their powdered jowls and immoderate narration; the chapped condition of their smiling as they spoke about the way the world had come to rash,

and how the ground would split apart
and spit up blobs of black and ooze and stinking
and the missionaries with their long tongues
and the steaming craters of the moon, and
the pastures of dead cattle already rotten within hours, the
beetles and the fungus spreading over,

the mayonnaise on a sandwich no one would ever eat, and the
babies with their hair tongues

like my baby here

like mine

More than the programs, my boy liked advertisements. He liked
to hiss or sing along in faction. At first I'd fast-forward through those
sent from late night, the 1-800 numbers with women moaning, but
then I began to find

that in those moments

he seemed most pleased,

most still and God-blessed,

and so I let him go on watching,

while outside the tides broke and swallowed cars,

and on the beaches the bloated continued rolling in, rotting even
in the sun's absence, clogged and ripped and lined with tumor.

These were other days, these ones prepared for us.

In these new days we no longer had to watch the mobs of wrecked
men with their machine guns, ten-thousand piled up on sheets of
concrete, the splintered knobs of bone so hushed,

the scum caked and ever-growing,

and all those thoughts of what for which I'd never get the time.

The words I could not somehow pass to baby. I'd wield a ball
and call its name, coo it cutely for my young one, B-A-L-L, and he'd
shriek back, KA-KEESH!

I'd put a finger to my forehead and say, MOMMY, and my child,
taller than me, went: PAWOOO PAWEEEE!

Stubborn, like his father, with the straight white teeth to match.

The things I knew he'd never be.

There was something ever coming, I said inside me, and it does
not have a name.

At night I locked the front door and watched for hours through
the peep. I locked the door that blocked the hallway and the one
leading to my room.

So many doors forever. There never were enough.

Each door had several locks.

One lock was combination. Another required keys. Another was
simple slide-latch. Another was strictly ornamental.

Another you could open by whispering the right thing to it at the
right time, which is the type of lock most humans have.

CATERPILLAR

They slung in wriggling ropes of segmented flesh: fat and spiny, bright with mold. Some squirmed big as my forearm. Some small enough to creep inside an ear. I'd never seen so much color. The leaves of trees were eaten, stranding craning skeletons in midsummer. Those who'd thought to brave the hail and made it now stayed indoors, their skins lesions with teethmarks. Bronze tanks patrolled the city. There was nightly concern over what to eat. You could imagine anything infested. Bugs showed up nestled in every crevice: in the bed sheets, in the oven. Some nights I just chewed the clumps out from my nails. I heard of an old man buried in his basement. I heard of young ladies smothered in their sleep. Fat cysts and burrowed nodules and red growths of sludge. No skin was safe. No simple evening. The national rate of suicide quadrupled. Sale of aspirin, rope, and razor blades became condemned. Other ways became more messy: one night a hundred dove off some skyscraper hotel. People began to wonder what _____ wanted. The airwaves filled with preaching: how to repent; what might save us; whom to look to; what to think. At night you could practically hear the low sound of our prayer, a billion lips all mumbling together into themselves. Meanwhile, by now, the cities lay covered in chrysalis, silken tents stretched across expressways, over homes. Our front door sealed shut with hive building. The cocoons crushed each time a thing moved. We waited. We blink-eyed through the night. In the end, the great unveiling: ten billion butterflies humming in the sun, fluttering so loud you couldn't think.

TELEVISION
MILK

Moths and blackbirds flooded the front yard. The trees uprooted, clogged with smoke. Someone was out there somewhere. We'd been waiting for forever. Downstairs the kids were naked, screaming with TV. They heard language in the bad transmission. In recent days it'd told them to shit straight on the floor. It told them to rip their clothes up, break our mirrors, lock me upstairs in the bedroom. My husband's scalp now hung from the ceiling along with several hundreds skins of local cats. In the long night you could hear them squealing. You could hear the children's chortle. They made cat meat casserole, cat meat salad, fur flambé. They fed me through the keyhole.

Dan and I had once felt love. We'd made three sons—blonde heads each, like his, six endless blue eyes. They began as sweet boys with careful manners. I did what I could do to keep them near. Before the schools closed I'd been very active in the PTA. Sometimes I subbed for their gym classes, which made them blush. The school's halls wormed with stabbing, maggots, grease, collapse, and homemade bombs. One boy in our neighborhood had his eye out. You should have seen what grew back in.

I didn't want my children to grow up frightened, unprepared. We enrolled them in karate. We bought them safety helmets, pugils, latex gloves and boots and masks. Dan wrote out lectures to read aloud before dinner, new forewarnings. His voice contained a smidge of squeak, a female banter, yet he still seemed to command the boys' attention. Sometimes he had to use his hands.

I'd always dreamt of becoming Mother. As a child myself I slept surrounded: a billion plastic babies, each with a name. I would make them kiss and lay against me. I'd whisper them my want. I'd been afraid, as I got older, that I'd never meet the proper man. That I'd end up old and alone with no one nowhere. In the night I clasped my hands. I prayed. I asked. I asked. I looked. I watched. I praised. I found. Though Dan hadn't been quite what I expected—balding and broke and older—he filled me full. He warmed my mind. He'd known the proper times to say the proper things.

In the end his blood had run all black and made another pattern on the carpet.

We'd made these babies despite the way at night the sky seemed drooping; the way sometimes the air hung thick as mud; so many buildings everywhere gone tilted, smothered, sucked into the earth or slung with sludge.

The TV static made our house vibrate. My teeth rattled at my brain.

The children let me out around the time for dinner and brought me downstairs to milk. It'd been several years since I'd nursed but somehow my glands could still produce. At first it'd taken some coaxing, a pinch, a punch, a howl, but eventually they had me gushing. I fed them each one after another, oldest to youngest, one by one.

Joey came on voracious, always starving. His skin was turning yellow. He blamed me for our trouble finding food. He gripped my left breast like a baseball.

Tum—awkward and fumbly, just near an age he might have begun to dream of women—he took my nipple in his mouth with his arms crossed over his chest, eyes anywhere but on me.

The youngest, Johnson, was losing his baby teeth so his was the easiest to handle. His mouth was soft and loose and nuzzled my areola without pain. Sometimes, when the other brothers had run off, he even let me hold him in the parcel of my lap and coo and clasp and hum a song. He'd always been the momma's boy beyond his brothers, the love-lump I could nudge.

That night, though, he couldn't keep me down. He kept hacking my milk across the carpet. His eyes were puffy. His teeth seemed slanted. He batted at my neck with fury in his eyes.

"Stop it," I said. "Be good."

He bit my nipple and I bled.

After feeding, we went into the living room and my boys tied me to the sofa. They'd caught Dan on the escape—*he hadn't warned me even with a premonition*—*he'd slipped into the night*. The bonds gripped tight across my forearms, causing flesh to web and redden. The TV went on screeching. Their pupils bulged in crystal puddles. The stinging waves of whir flooded and coursed all through my babies' eyes. I watched them watch till they were giddy-tired and then they came to sit around me on the floor. They demanded I tell stories of the way things were before.

As always, I took off on my childhood—how in the mornings behind my father's shed I'd walk until I couldn't see anything around me but long grass; how I'd lay down in the grass and look up at the ceiling of the sky and imagine being lifted off into the wide white flat nothing, my hair fluttering around my head, a mask, and every thought of scratch or ache or shudder washed out of me into air.

They didn't want to hear about that.

I went on about the circus—*the time I saw a man remove his head*—the zoo—*where babies grew in cages*—McDonald's—*god, their value meals, what now?*—I told them about anything I could think of that had been good once—anything that made me sting.

"Shut up and talk about TV," Tum said, slurring, his neck bulged fat with mold.

So I went on about my programs, before the channels all washed out. I told about our last game shows—*men in mud suits, grappling for food*—soap operas—*stretched to ribbons, the women bright orange and super-sewn*—the weather channel—*fat with layers, so many minor screens embedded into that one page, so small you couldn't see*—the nightly news—*I won't even say*—all the talk shows with people screaming who was whose daddy and eating pills and throwing fists.

This they liked. This made them rowdy. Tum clenched in fits and pinched my skin. The smaller two were crawling all against me. Joey bit into my wrists. They used their scissors on my hair and poked my stomach and threw glass against the wall. They blindfolded me and made me touch things and try to guess what they were—hot kettle, steak knife, razor, something pudding-soft about which they'd only giggle. With a gag and bag over my head, they spread me on the floor and fed again.

Through all of this I did my best to remain still. I thought of nothing. I was tired.

We were tired, I guess I mean.

Through the next days, locked in the bedroom, I began to try again—to try to wish or want, and yet in want of nothing, as there was nothing I could taste. The space inside the small room we'd once used for a nursery had grown engorged with dirt, the walls and carpet frittered full with raspy holes threaded by tapeworms and aphids, eating. I'd yank on wallpaper to let the looser dustings shake so there'd be something I could chew. My tongue took to the texture but my belly would not stop screaming, and the bug matter hung in gristle, my stomach so weak it couldn't grind. I could feel my offspring moving elsewhere. I could feel the crawl behind my eyes.

The old ceiling sat around me. The new ceiling: a smudged sky. In the idea of those unbent stars still drooling—the false hope of short-lived water rain—I began to convince myself there would be something somewhere some time again. I had scars all up my forearms. Larvae in my hair. My teeth ached. And deeper, in my organs, something else I couldn't put a name to. Other eyes behind my eyes.

When the sound of scissors filled my forehead, I swallowed air until they wore away. I would rock and lick the salt of my kneecaps and laugh aloud and remember math. I'd been good at that crap sometime. I counted days in further scratches on my forearms. I heard awful noises in the walls. Above the static, a high pitched squealing. The bang of hammers. Thump of weight. I called the boys for water. I called the boys to come. I called and called and called until my voice broke my throat.

Through the window, too small for my body, I saw they'd took to piling our books and baubles in the backyard. The kitchen curtains. Their baby blankets. Grandma's afghan. They'd learned some kind of dance. Out of the wood Dan had used to build a treehouse, they'd made an altar, tall as me.

Over time the room got smaller. The air felt liquid. I fell thin.

In the eaves I sensed a groaning.

In the floor where once I'd held my babies one by one and hummed, set in the wood I found a mouth. A man's mouth—warm and easy. I felt his gender in the bristle of his bridge and the texture of his breath. By taste I knew it wasn't Dan—Dan's mouth crammed with rotting molars and gold loam. I could not remember other men. Yet when I came near enough this man would whisper, his voice ruined and raspy, beehive flutter. He mostly said only one thing, a name, I think, though nothing held. He would repeat until the words became just words, until even what short sleep came for me was slurred. To shut him up I'd spit between them, what dry saliva I could manage, and the lips would shrivel, bring a hum. You could hear him suck for hours, my taste some nourishment, a fodder. But soon enough again the wishing, formed in hymn.

Finally I took the dirt that would have been my dinner and meshed the lips over to make the floor full flush and proper. Then the world again was hushed and far off. I began to teach myself the words I'd need when things returned: the yes and please and bless you. The ouch and why and I remember. I tried to find Dan's voice in my head, but the sounds from outside and there in me brought a blur: the electric storms, the shaking, the bright nights, the itch, the rip. I continued to continue to try. I waited longer and the trying became a thing worn like a hairpin in my heart. Or more aptly like my fingernails—nearly an inch each by now, growing out of me some crudded yellow. In time I'd become sly and slouched enough to eat those goddamned slivers of myself. But before that I'd wish the mouth back. I'd lap the dirt and find a hole. One tiny nozzle down to nowhere, black no matter how loud into it I'd beg or bark or sing.

■

In the yard now the trees were burning. Grass was burning. The sky was full of ruptured light. I stood with my face pressed against the picture window, my face obscured by the house's bug-hung panes. I beat the door until my fists hurt. Through the vents I sniffed the ash. My stomach grappled, squealing high notes. They'd crushed my glasses. I couldn't see. I rummaged in my purse for lint or crumbs to chew. My purse now a bag of crap—still I couldn't let it go, this bag of who I'd been—I carried it with me waiting for some moment in which the world would blink: the cell phone towers long dead and voiceless; paper money *blah*; the car's battery long excavated so the boys would have power for their TV.

Wrapped in tissue, I found the tweezers I'd once used to tend Dan's back. The skin across his shoulders, in those last years, had begun to grow a rind. The hairs came out blackened and endless, enough to knit a bed. In the evenings, while the boys slept, I'd had him lay down on the carpet in the foyer, and I'd straddle him as Mother, and I'd pick those damn things clean. I picked and picked and felt their popping. No matter how many came, I kept it up, while below me Dan squirmed and grumbled and said for this whole thing please to all be over.

On the floor now I bit and winced and sucked the tweezer metal— felt something real—his taste.

Somewhere later in some blackness I found my youngest up above me. At first it seemed he floated. His head was wet. He had black crap all around his mouth—something gunky, runny, rancid. He was breathing hard and sweating. I pulled him down and let him suck my breast and he was calmer then, designed. For several seconds he let me hold him curled in a J there on the carpet. I found his arms engraved with diagrams and runic symbols, long lines of creeping dot. His back was run with lumps and oozing. His hair matted, clogged with sore. He let me kiss him where it hurt. He let me say his name in certain ways. He let me come with him back downstairs into the kitchen, where I took ice and cleaned his face. I combed the crap out of his lashes. I put a cube inside his mouth. Through the window the backyard glowed. I heard the other boys out there chanting in some rhythm.

The cords in Johnson's neck pumped with flex. I could see his heartbeat, gushed and stuttered. I felt the tremor of his nostrils. He looked at me funny.

"You're not supposed to be out yet, Mommy," he said, rasping. "We aren't ready." His eyes were glassy, boggled, flat.

I rifled through my purse to find the photos tucked in the fake leather slits of my old wallet. I showed him a shot of us with some bald mall Santa. The fat man's lap a wide seat for the boys, their faces unsmeared with these new days, their cheeks rose pink and full of breath. All this a month before the mall filled up with sludge and the sun went hyper-violet and the grass squirmed and the water swam inside itself. These other older days were ones I could remember. Whens to want.

Johnson smudged a finger on the print.

"Who is that one?" he said. He was pointing at himself.

"That's you, my dear, my darling," I told him. "When you were just a tiny boy."

He looked confused. He pointed at the tanned and unblemished captured image of some younger husk of me.

"Who is that one?"

I felt my size.

"That's me. Your mother. Who loves you more than all. Who would give and give and give and give."

He took the photo from me, stumbling. His eyeballs jerked and spun. He wiped the grime from his mouth across his face. He looked at me. He was in there.

"No," he said. "You're lying."

I told him how I'd never lie. How all I wanted was to have my boys together all around me, loving. He snorted through his nostrils. He looked into the slathered backyard with his brothers: the rash the steam the broiling. I felt the roof just slightly shift. Johnson looked at me again, something grunting, an idea hung between his lips. He kind of grinned to flash his teeth, the greening grubby things— they'd used their toothpaste on my eyes. One short, overtly hairy hand came up through the air to point.

"Mommy?" he said. "You?"

"Yes, yes me, my dear," I said, breathing the moment. "My sweetest Johnson. My precious baby."

His whole head clouded. His soft skin bluing. He cricked his neck. He pinched his fingers deep back in his mouth, pulled something out, and ate it. He shook his head horrendous.

"Not a baby," he said. "I am fire. I know who you are now. I can smell everywhere you've been."

He reached and dug his nails into my arm. My blood bubbled in splotches. Johnson's tongue was white. I felt something seeping sink all through me as he pulled me hard toward the back door, through the smudgy glass of which I could see now shapes moving in and at the light. Several massive crosses propped erect and glowing, crowed beneath the sky that seemed to open. What wasn't burning lurched with insect, the grass and limbs and hills and neighbors' houses washed in crease. The air itself was sweat. This was what had happened.

I ripped my arm away from my youngest and fell back onto the cracking kitchen floor. I skittered to stand up as he watched me, still holding the photo crumpled in his hand. His eyes burst veined and raw. The smear of his etchings and bruises seemed to form a pattern. He shrieked out for his brothers. His tone was crystal, wounded as we were. The house around us shuddered

I turned from my son.

I ran out through the kitchen's side door into the garage. My stomach swished, my knees gone goofy. The night was wrecked and drooping. The air was eaten through with smear holes. Large patches of blue mold hung on the burped crust of the moon—the moon that in recent months had grown smaller, sucked away by something much larger snuck behind it. The air was hot and made me sneeze. My blood. My blood. I ran into the forest half-blinded, thumbed by branches that made long scratches on my skin. I could hear the boys behind me. They whooped, calling out my maiden name. They put inflection in their voices to make it sound in trouble, hurt, causing a receding part of me to stir. I plugged my ears and thought of elsewhere. I thought of wrapping my arms around a younger Dan, my heart wet and drumming through my shirt.

I ran until I couldn't see.

I ran until my brain was lather.

I ran until I felt the bottom fall out of me, drumming, and tumbled facedown on the earth.

Somewhere in the dead grass between the sanitation yard that'd once been a school lot and the rotten playground where Dan and I used to bring them through several summers, I knew I could not go on. I fell and scuffed my soft hands and rolled around with dirt. In this new dirt I still could not find the mouth—*what had I become?* My skin had opened up in several places, the center of me oozed. The smoke from our small house plumed in odd tufts on the horizon.

I waited for the boys.

I waited that they'd catch up and lift my body, carry me on their young backs to our home. To the small house where they'd grown up. Where I'd loved them and they'd eaten and we'd breathed. Such air we'd had together. The night was sticky. I was cold. Blood gushed down my forearms. Something throbbing at my forehead from all directions. All I could see was straight above me. Above and on and on and into nothing. I felt dumb for having run. I felt weird warmth brimming in my eyes. My gone eyes. My warbled wanting. My boys needed me to feed. They needed something like the rest of us. They'd had no great chance to change. Such long, bombed days of wait and television. Such backward years; such years to come. I would get up in a moment. I'd go to them and say their names. I'd fill their mouths and kiss their earlobes. The days would wash. The boys would listen. The sky would come uncombed and gleaming. I could sense it. I could seem.

STATIC

The earth had learned to scratch its back. In massive columns same as what we'd seen on TV during our worse storms, stretched check-pattern, warbled spatter. As well, the sound of a billion needles wheedling, tearing their tips against the grain. Sometimes I could hear laugh tracks buried under the floorboards, wedged deep under the sod. Somewhere down there was my father. His knuckled rapped against the beams. I began to feel everything inside me at once humming. I felt my organs hiss alive: the static replicated in me. When my mouth opened, it came out. The vibration cracked my mirrors. It split the foundations of my soft skull. It made me giggle just a bit. I couldn't keep a hold on as through the windows I saw the wide scrim that for years had nestled me into sleep—the gray/white/black transmission from gone channels, wavelengths no one had thought to walk.

THE GOWN FROM MOTHER'S STOMACH

The mother ate thread and lace for four weeks so that her daughter would have a gown. She was tired of not being able to provide her daughter with the things many other girls took for granted. Their family was poor and the mother's fingers ached with arthritis so she couldn't bring herself to sew. Instead she chewed the bed sheets until they were soft enough to swallow. She bit the curtains and gnawed the pillow. With one wet finger she swiped the floor for dust. *God will knit it in my womb like he did you*, she murmured. *When you wear it you will blind the world.* She refused to listen to reason. She ate toilet tissue and sheets of paper and took medication that made her constipated. She stayed in bed instead of sitting for dinner. *Carrots don't make a dress*, she croaked. Her stomach grew distended. She began having trouble standing up. Her hair fell out and she ate that too. She ripped the mattress and munched the down. She ate the clothing off her body. The father was always gone. He worked day and night to keep food the mother wasn't eating on the table. When he did get home he was too tired to entertain the daughter's pleas to make the mother stop. *Such a tease, that woman*, he said in his sleep, already gone. *Such a card.* Because her mother could no longer walk, the daughter spent the evenings by the bedside listening to rambles. The mother told about the time she'd seen a bear. *A bear the size of several men*, she said. *There in the woods behind our house, when I was still a girl like you.* The mother had stood in wonder watching while the bear ate a whole deer. It ate the deer's cheeks, its eyes, its tongue, its pelt. It ate everything but the antlers. The mother had waited for the bear to leave so she could take the antlers home and wear them, but the bear had just gone on laying, stuffed, smothered in blood. The mother swore then—her eyes grew massive in the telling—the bear had spoken. It'd looked right at the mother and said, quite casual, *My god, I was hungry.* Its voice was gorgeous, deep and groaning. The mother could hardly move. *I didn't know bears could talk*, she said finally, and the bear had said, *Of course we can. It's just that no one ever takes the time to hear. We are old and we are lonely and we have dreams you can't imagine.* Over the next six days the mother continued growing larger. Her eyes began to change. Her belly swelled to six times its normal size. Dark patchwork showed through her skin. Strange ridges on her abdomen in maps. Finally the daughter called a doctor. He came and looked and locked the door behind him. Through the wood the daughter could hear her mother moan. A wailing shook the walls. Some kind of grunt or bubble. The doctor emerged with bloody hands. He was sweating, sickly pale. He left without a bill. In the bedroom, the air stunk sweet with rotten melon. The gown lay draped over the footboard. It was soft and glistening, full of color—blue like the afghan that covered her parents' bed—white like the spider's webs hung from the ceiling—gray and orange like their two fat tabbies—green like the pine needles past the window—yellow and crimson like how the sun rose—gold like her mother's blinkless eyes.

■

The daughter wore the gown thereafter. It fit her every inch. It sung in certain lighting. She liked to suck the cuff against her tongue. There was a sour taste, a crackle. She could hear her mother murmur when she lay a certain way. The father, fraught by what he'd lost unknowing, began staying home all day. He stood in the kitchen and ate food for hours. He ate while crying, mad or mesmerized. He didn't answer when the daughter spoke. Sometimes he shook or nodded, but mostly he just chewed. Most days the daughter took to walking as far from the house as she could manage. The gown made her want to breathe new air. She'd go until her feet hurt or until the sun went low. When it rained the gown absorbed the water. It guzzled her secret sweat. She got up earlier, patrolled. She wanted to see something like her mother had, like the bear, so that one day she'd have a story for a daughter. She saw many things that you or I would gape at—two-headed cattle, lakes of insect, larvae falling from the sky—all things to her now everyday. The earth was very tired. The daughter found nothing like a talking bear. She wondered if her mother had been lying or smeared with fever. At school the other children threw sharp rocks. They ripped the daughter's gown and held their noses. The daughter quit her classes. She walked until her feet bled. Her father didn't notice. Like the mother, he took on size. His jowls hung fat in ruined balloons. He called for the mother over mouthfuls. Her name was SARAH. The way it came out sounded like HELLO. The daughter couldn't watch her father do the same thing her mother had. She decided to go on a long walk—longer than any other. She touched her father on the forehead and said goodbye. She walked up the long hill in her backyard where in winter she had sledded. It hadn't been cold enough for snow in a long time but she could still remember the way her teeth rattled. She remembered losing the feeling in her body. Now every day was so warm. She swore she'd sweat an ocean. She walked through the forest well beyond dark. The gown buzzed in her ears. It buzzed louder the further from home she went. She kept going. She slept in nettles. She dreamt of sitting with her parents drinking tea and listening to her tell about all the things she would soon see. She dreamt of reversing time to watch her parents grow thinner, younger, while the earth grew new and clean. She walked by whim. She tread through water. She saw a thousand birds, saw lightning write the sky, the birds falling out in showers. The world was waning. The sky was chalk. She felt older every hour. She had no idea she'd come full circle to her backyard when she found the bear standing at a tree. It was huge, the way her mother had said, *the size of several men*. It was reaching after leaves. It sat up when it heard her. It looked into her eyes. *Hello, bear*, she said, rasping. *It's nice to finally meet you.* The bear stood up and moved toward her, its long black claws big as her head. The collar of her dress had pulled so tight she found it hard to speak: *What do you dream, bear? I will listen.* She didn't flinch as the bear came near and put its paw upon her head. It battered at her and she giggled. It pulled her to its chest. She didn't feel her head pop open. She didn't feel her heart squeeze wide. The bear dissembled her in pieces. The bear ate the entire girl. It ate her hair, her nails, her shoes and bonnet. It ate the gown and ate her eyes. Inside the bear the daughter could still see clearly. The bear's teeth were mottled yellow. Inside its stomach, abalone pink. The color of the daughter became something soft— then something off, then something fuzzy, then something like the gown, immensely hued; then she became a strange fluorescence and she exited the bear—she spread across the wrecked earth and refracted through the ocean to split the sky: a neon ceiling over all things, a shade of something new, unnamed.

TEETH

I felt it formed in chatter: voices borne in the enamel. The sky sent
teeth from cougar, leopard, shark, snake, kitten, cow, human, bear,
dog, alligator, crocodile, deer, rodent, camel, zebra, turtle, rabbit,
horse, and wolf. And bigger things we hadn't quite imagined, teeth
that wouldn't fit inside a car. The massive incisors bashed through
buildings. They impaled people huddled in their dens. They clipped
the ground and erupted waist-deep craters large enough in which
one could lie down. In the light you could hardly stand to look for
all the glinting, the masked back-rattle. You couldn't step without
incision. The aching stretched our gums. I told the young ones how
some new fairy had dropped her payload in mid-flight. The children
wouldn't wink. At this point we'd lost ways of sentiment. Overhead
there hung a thing that seemed to want us nowhere. I couldn't help
but want to stay under. I couldn't remember anyone I'd ever met.
The names of people once relations hid chipped, minor abrasions
into my brain. I'd had a mother, I knew, and someone besides her.
I'd had people who would talk. But these days were so overloaded,
so crusted over and back-bent, I didn't know what else to speak of
when I spoke into the brusque remainder of my household, into the
crooks that hadn't yet been demolished. I touched my own teeth
with my soft tongue and wondered how long before they'd be the
ones that rained down and ripped us open.

SEABED

Randall had a head the size of several persons' heads—a vast seething bulb with rotten hair that shined under certain light. Several summers back he'd driven to a bigger city where smarter men removed a hunk out of his skull. They'd said the cyst grew from the wires hung above the house. Randall's son hadn't ended up so well off. The crap ate through the kid's whole cerebrum. Radiation. Scrambled cells. *One had to be mindful of these things in these days*, the doctors said. Now, though, with the woman gone and the baby dead, Randall kept on living in that old house with the mold curtains where his guilt breathed in the walls. He lugged the kid's tricycle all over, the handlebars shrieking with rust on account of how he even brought it in the bath.

The streets were ruined that evening as he sulked half-cocked among the light. There'd been a parade at 3:00 p.m. for the Governor's next wedding, a celebration of his legal promise to a whore he'd got caught pants-down with by the paper—therein, stoned on flashbulbs, the elected had sworn the fraggy dyke his betrothed: all six foot four of her, thickly mustached, tattooed every inch. Like most days, though, Randall slept to dusk, so that by the time he got up and fit his pants on and cleaned the dead birds off the porch—those fuckers fell all hours due to, again, the power lines, another stunner in the long line of hell that kept him up—the crepe had been unraveled. The trombones pumped and champagne popped. The whole town seemed to have cleared out. There were no sedans, no street sweepers, no bastards out on the club porch, where most days by now they rallied barking, randy for date rape.

Randall headed on along the strip where wheel wells from parade floats scarred the dirt. Folks had tricked their cars into makeshift barges, spurting confetti and huge balloons. They'd built a twenty-foot high reproduction of the Governor out of mud and chicken wire, which for days had towered up into the sky outside the trailer known as City Hall—a multicolor monolith, in minor silhouette of god. Seeing such a thing made Randall wonder his own quadrupled replica might look like—zonked out eyes as tunnels, a skull so big it blotted out the sky. In school they'd called him Lump Skull, Fat Face.

They'd smeared his name on bathroom walls with shit. They'd made him stand profiled under the monkey bars so they could swing down from each end and kick his eyes. On and on in that way for years until one day in shop class he'd tried to stick his neck into the band saw. After that he'd been expelled, ripped from the rosters, which at first had seemed a gift—though at home things weren't much different. Randall's parents were good-looking and ashamed. At night they locked their room.

Randall hadn't shuddered when the mold collapsed their bedroom ceiling. He could at last now, he thought, be alone.

Thereafter, though, among the damp halls, the house hummed with the phantoms of those it'd claimed. In the squished air Randall could hear all three, the folks, the baby, taking turns shaking the ceiling, breaking lamps. He could hear them clawing inside his grubby mattress. However long he lay, there was no rest. Randall prayed soon the mold would pile in on him too, deep enough no one could dig him up.

In the dirt, Randall passed the skin and nail salon where on weekends he liked to watch the girls prance out with their new flesh. He hadn't sniffed a woman since the dead child's mother left to meet a man she'd met on a 1-900 party line. Randall imagined her in wider rooms now, bloated with new chub from further births. She likely had a lot of other people in her life.

There was no one in the P.O. None in the laundromat, the frazzled gravel lot.

When the road ended where the town did, Randall continued walking on. He slogged up the mulch ridge ruptured with ant dirt into the smidge of half-dead sun-damaged trees. The days were lasting longer lately. Instead of fourteen hours, the sun would stay for sixteen, twenty. Some nights night never came.

Randall trudged until his breath stung. He turned to look back from where he'd come. White spurs of lightning stung at certain roofs. Randall's stomach threw itself against his inner meat. He sat down in dirt and stared.

In the light slurring behind him he watched the streets eject a thing that moved. He couldn't tell for sure, at first: a shimmer, conjured cogs of spreading heat. He squinted through the stutter until it made a girl. She followed the hill the same way he had, approaching slow, but locked on course—as if she'd been sent to greet him, or he her, there in this absence.

Soon she stood right there beside, skin from skin by inches. Through clotted locks he saw her eyes slit flat over cheeks somehow newly bruised. He recognized the dress—a smock of several garish colors, picked to bits. He couldn't tell if he smelled himself or her. She sat beside him, knee to knee.

"My father isn't in the kitchen," she said, blinkless. "He's not in the whole house."

Randall stood up and shook his head off. He stretched as if she wasn't there. Above, the sky made bubble, blurred with humid grog. Several dozen black birds circled above the town in halo— no, *not a halo*—a living crust. In recent weeks he'd watched them swoop down and nip old women on the bonnet, their feathers chock with nit.

When he started back in for the city, the girl fell in behind, keeping close through the wrecked light until again they stood among street windows reflecting the outside on itself. The panes heat-warbled in their framework, the glass again becoming sand.

Every so often, the girl offered interjection, questions with no answers Randall knew—

Where are people?

Will they be back?

Why aren't we also gone?

Who's the trike for?

What has made your head so huge?

Randall walked in silence, squeezing the puckered plastic of his son's tricycle's handles—worn thin by his own fingers, not the child's. He'd tried several times to ride it: his enormous knees and legs tangled alone among the metal in the night.

Other hours of certain solitary evenings Randall heard his father talking through the house. Most of the speech, to Randall, swam in blather—BUGMERMENNUNMMEM USSIS LUMMMM. Some words he understood—*every inch of every inch of every thing you see is fucked. Might as well come ahead and muck it. Put your big head through the wall.*

Sometimes the boy joined in—his son who'd yet to use a voice, now stretched heavy, echoed, spooled in ache—mostly just repeating one thing over and over—*What else could you have done?*

Through the past weeks they'd been louder.

Randall's mother never said a word.

Randall felt the girl's eyes on him now, her stuttered breathing, the film that made windows of her skin.

The birds had redoubled overhead. They circled a small circumference just above the city, black. There must have been hundreds now, suspended—a ceiling waiting to rain shit. The wings' crick and neon cawing filled air the same way their feathers choked the light.

The girl tried to take Randall's hand and their sweat-flushed fingers zapped.

The birds stayed just above as they moved forward. The sky had flushed a ruddy color, more blood than regal, thunder in some long drum roll slow and low all through.

Randall walked a little faster, his fat legs and ass meat rubbing, warm.

He could not stop thinking how if he walked long enough, he'd make fire. Spontaneous human combustion—his whole head set ablaze—his frazzled locks in wicks lighting the no-night firmament alive.

Behind he heard the girl there breathing, trying to keep up.

He stopped and knelt in the dirt to untie and tie his shoe. She tried again to take his hand.

Though he still slipped away, this time he sighed and scratched the moles sunk in his back. He put the tricycle down between them.

"There," he said. "Ride that then. For a minute."

She sat on the cracked seat and adjusted her thin legs. He couldn't see her smile for all the hair.

They went to where the runoff ditches came together, where once the local council each year planted mums. The concrete was cracking open. The veins coagulated into lines, leading along the black, bump-battered surface down the gully to the clump of green most locals called a forest. The trees' limbs had lost their baggage, the cells and skins all wilted, limping down. Even through the mesh of tree crap, Randall could hear the birds above.

The tricycle's bald wheels ground against the gravel behind him, throwing off short showers of spark.

The suffered branches made a hall.

On and on with walking, Randall's stomach queased from so much motion in their air. He named the first things that came to mind, his own series of questions, spoke into his head—

What was new now?

When was ugly?

How had the meat aligned our eyes?

Who had been here?

Who was coming?

What could anybody want?

After each he ground his teeth and tried to keep his tongue still, but the words slid on his gums and worked his lungs open, filled him with some color heavy even on the light enclosed.

On the far side of the forest, Randall realized they were headed for the dump—a half-mile-deep gorge just outside the town where people went to ditch their junk. For years it'd all been building up there, squat in the middle of what more fervent regions might have made a landmark. They could have sequestered it off, got government funding and a proclamation, brought fat tourists from all over to buy tickets to a sight to see. Instead they fed it their condom wrappers, their plastic linings, their lint-trap crap and old foil. Randall could smell the sum there from his bedroom when the wind blew the right way.

In the sky above, slow cycling color, the birds skronked at their approach. Randall could feel each of the thousands of tiny eyes glared down upon him, wanting him forward. He heard the innard questions cannoned, cawing, making lesions on his throat.

What is who doing ever?

What's the best thing?

Blassmix buntum veep?

They called him on along the hill, still up the half-paved path that ended not just in sanitation, but in voltage—the machines birthing all the wires hung in nest over his house. Even before they'd reached the lip of the drop-off Randall could see the steel-gray multi-paneled mongoloid of boxy mass, the unknown smog and slither burping up to join the broth of skying clog above. The air all stunk of fire, shit and oil and liquidated hair. He'd grown accustomed after years of inhale, but this, much closer, made him choke.

At his side, hunched on the tricycle, the girl pulled the neckline of her dress over her mouth, her eyes already bloodshot, the veins blistering to knots.

From the top ridge of the chasm lip, they saw together down into the gorge.

At the bottom, piled among the trash, sat the grand finale of the Governor's parade. The crepe left crashed and punctured. Bloating bodies squashed around old coupes, their metal crumpled, battered, caved. Whole truckbeds full of people toppled—people other people'd loved. Women Randall had ogled with gross wanting. The men he'd spent endless nights with pounding shots with, fly-licked blood now flooding from their mouths. Even the mammoth Governor replica whipped to pieces, its neck snapped and elbows bent. Not far, the Governor himself lay ripped, his new woman jackknifed at his side. Randall could not quit his brain from seeing each body somersaulting one after another. Their last air coming out or stuck inside them, hung.

Overhead the birds still hovered, half a billion screeching, shitting, hiding light.

The girl stood beside him mouth half open. He couldn't even find the nerve to turn her head.

In his mind: *The birds. The birds.*

A funny feeling came over him then—a tingle ripping through his fat. Looking down onto the wreckage, Randall felt the sudden impulse to go on and jump off, to throw himself into the chasm with the wind of the birds' wings riffling his hair. He kicked a rock and watched it topple, pocking some ex-neighbor's exposed skull between the eyes. It was only by some scummy nod of knowing that he didn't just go on.

Above, the legions watched, clocked in his ears. The black abrasion of the sky behind them now, made of all color, was on the verge of waking, breach.

Randall put a hand against his heavy skull and lard-rung forehead, the last door against the noise—the same fat fucking head he'd almost scratched off a hundred times. He could feel those goddamn questions for which again he had no answer, his brain into a lock they had the key to, so much scrape—

WHO WAS COMING

WHAT COULD ANYBODY WANT

Muffled as they were, he could not quit it. Scrims of new night flushed his numb. His son's head in the heavens, begging. His father behind, eyes brightened, wide. Randall covered at his holes. He turned toward the girl. Her eyes were wetter now, her skin pulled taut, showing their veins. The birds weren't inside her, Randall could see that, though he could not name what it was that kept them out.

The girl pointed past him in the gorge rip, somehow aimed at one man bloated on top of several others, his black hair thick the way the girl's was, his lips stretched and pleased, wide beyond their size. She nodded, blinking, forced her eyes closed, pulled her arms into her dress. She got off the trike, the cushion sticking. She wheeled the wheels to Randall and fixed his hand around the metal. So much rust. The once white grips now gray. He nudged the frame once with his right foot, again, again, until it tottered off the gorge edge. Below, it made no sound.

He turned back toward the girl, his whipped eyes brimming in the treble. He couldn't move yet. He tried to see her. She nodded once and stepped toward. The birds lurched with her movement. Screeching. She didn't blink. She reached.

This time when her hand hit his, he held it. It felt like his son's once, during those few months he'd had a chance to feel—the palm pudgy and dampened, the fingers fragile, warm.

With the child, he turned around to face the forest, from the bird sound, from the sun.

■

They'd been walking for a week then. When the girl felt faint or winded, Randall would hoist her up. He didn't like to stop for very long for any reason. He didn't know where they were going, though he knew there had to be somewhere else from where they were— miles from any other city, miles from where they'd come.

In the blanched road they crossed dog carcasses wearing tags engraved with phone numbers, family names. Craters lined with white mud. Burnholes in the earth. The birds that had followed in fat flocks for the first few days had by now fallen from the sky, or disseminated after other things.

Randall let the girl eat leaves and roots and soft paper and anything preserved or clean enough. He had her chew her hair and nails for protein. When she asked what he would eat, he rubbed his gut. "So much saved up I could go forever," he'd say in smile, though he knew if they didn't find good food and water soon, they would wither, slump, and die.

They continued on together in a straight line beneath the scratched lid of the sky. The sun stayed stuck ahead unblinking. It did not wax or wane or become obscured by clouds or disappear for night. The surplus glow affected Randall's vision. The ground and air lightened several shades. Slim spheres of heat moved in his margin—gaudy, blistered blobs of nothing. Inside his head he saw slow color, melted, morphed, and neon-blinked. Sometimes the colors formed his son—two blistered eyes behind his own eyes. His brain burped and gobbled, wriggling.

He could hardly think of what had been. He said his name over and over under horse breath to keep his mouth shape from forgetting, but soon even those familiar syllables went marred. His skin began to feel taut and made of leather. It peeled in layers. Itched his blood.

He tried to make the girl stay wrapped in a tarp torn from a camper, but she kept letting it slide off—she wanted to see where they were going, though she seemed to know he didn't know.

When they weren't talking, which was mostly, she hummed in glitches, cuts of hymn he'd never heard. She'd insist he hold her hand.

They crossed expressways with concrete cracking, large gaps woke in the median where the cars had skidded off, their windows sweltered obscure with condensation, airbags deployed and flaccid, popped. Smoke and ash hung on the air in streamered fuzz. They passed long fields where all the grass had died and ruptured black. Where there'd been forests once the trees had fallen over rotten and turned half to mush against the ground, the dirt riddled infertile with threadworms and microbes, small creatures burrowing spored homes. Drainage ditches gathered backed up with yellowed foam that didn't give when it was kicked, though the stench was almost liquid.

Sometimes the sky would open up. Storms would appear out of nowhere, without thunder or a cloud. The only thing that didn't rain was water. Lather. Crickets. Lesions. Seed. Sand drenched in thin torrential pillars, poured from above by erupted hourglasses. Blades of grass came whipped by wind and sliced the thin skin of Randall's wrecked head. Peapods, pine straw, even plastic—sometimes they had to dig themselves out of what'd come down. Worse were the insects—gnat, mosquito, aphid—wriggling at their eyes. They picked the shit out of one another's hair.

They hid under bridges or in carports that'd been abandoned. They made lean-tos out of rotten saplings, formed pillows from dead leaves. Often within minutes the girl snoozed soundly no matter what surrounded, her small head humming; Randall only ever tossed. He ripped his hair out in fat folds and threw up. He felt birds rutting in his stomach. His brain fizzled, swelling out.

He figured the sooner he did not remember, the sooner he would sleep.

The girl kept singing, making noise. She didn't seem to notice what they'd come through. She announced what she'd be when she grew older. An astronaut, she said. A breadmaker. Randall often could not catch his breath.

They saw ruin and rocks and shit and stinging in long plates of earth congealed.

They saw whole buildings made to dander—where there'd once been people, now burned black and shrunken.

Sometimes Randall convinced himself they'd fallen into a repeating circle—a long whirred loop they'd never leave—every inch around them lurched the same, what with the stagnant sun ruining all bearing and the anthills. He didn't try to understand.

They moved across the state, its borders pummeled, the land flattened out, awaiting flood.

They uncovered liquid cupped in gutters and strained it through his shirt and drank.

The girl's skin turned soft and pasty. It snowed off her back in flakes. Randall stayed thankful they didn't have a mirror.

They came upon the coast.

Even there standing on the bleached sand, Randall stood and sucked his tongue. He couldn't imagine they'd made it that far. He hadn't seen the beach since he went once as a child, afraid to step on the sand for fear of the clam holes, that they'd come up and rip into his feet.

Now they found the water missing. Where once there'd been multitudes half-naked, bathing, sunbathing, the shore was swarmed with dragonflies. Their blue bodies hovered, buzzing, looking for further things that'd died: they'd already stripped the meat off of the beached trout, the scales of salmon husked off, glinting light.

The sand cracked beneath their feet. The shore sat scummed over and pile-driven down, pale combs of foam dried at the farthest point where water'd lapped. Cracked shells of land-stuck jellies and uncased conch flesh sat overcooking, dried out, picked apart. Whole gulls with their skulls pecked in and post-ravaged by sand mites and worms.

The sun had drunk the ocean.

The sun more rapt than ever overhead.

Randall's eyes could not keep their focus as the girl picked ahead among the wreckage. She fished sand dollars out of murk pools. She giggled, gaffed, hummed la-la-la. Tucked in the half-smashed ruins of some sand palace, she found a transistor buried up to its antennae. She dug it out and cleaned the speaker. She wiped the corroded batteries and licked the dials white, straightened the wires with her teeth. Soon she had the half-ruined thing alive, burping static broken by occasional squeals of incoming sound.

She skittered between the stations, searching to match the song set in her head. Randall didn't have the heart to tell her it was useless, that nothing clear would come through now—how all those cryptic wavelengths once transmitting now were just more radiation. It made her happy just the same.

With nowhere else to go and under such stench, they continued on along the seabed. They walked out where before the water had been, the stretch of crunching sand endless for miles. Randall shuddered as they passed close to where once the tides would have lapped over their heads—for years in sleep he'd found himself stranded in such black; the miles and miles of unknown depth culling him under, full of grime.

They saw the dead all fuzzed and sunning. Whole fish schools. A swollen porpoise. Schools of jellyfish beat to vaseline. The seaweed knotted in fat brown scalps and punched with rash.

In small landlocked pockets they found tiny lidless fish clustered in barnacles and eaten through by mites.

Further out, there came another kind of wreckage: moored boats and ocean liners, rotting and picked apart by weather. Men's skins lifted from their bodies. The whitewashed limbs of enormous swimming things held encrusted in the matted sand.

They continued in a short trench out into the heart of where the wet had been.

The phantom waves seemed to lap at Randall's head. He breathed air that once would have been liquid. He kept looking back behind him, waiting to see the sea come back, enfolding. The brine filling his nostrils. The water wrapped around his face.

The girl messed with the transmitter's signals near him, squelching. Certain frequencies ached his teeth, CHPCHRRAKRAK. The bulbs and wires screamed. Randall imagined those same signals invisible in the air around him, licking up against his skin, the same way they'd ruined his son: the errored flood of digits soldered to nothing, wormed into the flesh of the baby's head; how the head's molecules had formed clusters in reaction, spreading out, a blooming fist.

As they got further from the shore ground, the sand began to level out. The refuse became more sparse or deeper buried. The ground made one long blur in all directions, its one bland color stretched. The sun stayed put, enchanting. Randall stared into it, forcing his eyes against the blink. He let the light wash his vision hazy. In seconds he couldn't see where he was going; he let his stumbling lead them further, the heat washing in boggled machination behind his face. He chewed just slightly on his ached tongue, imagined steak. He could hear the girl veering around him, lit by the cracked transistor's bleep. She was to his left, then right; behind then way on; then somehow overhead. He felt overheated. He felt multi-pronged and run through. He continued on regardless, warbling. He blew a saliva bubble and it popped softly on his lips.

When he could see, he saw a house—ranch-style, dull orange, three-bed two-and-a-half-bath, there in the stomach of the land.

Randall looked, and looked again. It was not apparent from the condition of the house that it had been underwater. The flat sheen of the old paint shone in the new light. He and the girl stood there before it, blinking. The large-paned windows glared and gleamed.

The speaker between them went ABEEEEEEZE.

There was a welcome mat and a tall chimney that stretched so far into the sky Randall couldn't tell at all where it ended and where something else began. Several plastic children's toys were left scattered in the sand yard. There was a swing set and a bench. There was a two-door garage inside which two twin black vehicles sat silent.

Randall touched the vinyl siding and found it warm and flat, undisappearing. He crossed the sand yard up the short stoop to the front door. There was a texture to the stair steps, razed in a pattern that crossed his eyes. He climbed the steps and rang the bell. The toning chimed inside the house, one long whole note that resounded, then was over. Nothing moved. No eye appeared inside the spyglass. No footsteps. Randall knocked three times with all his knuckles. He tried the knob and found it locked. The doorframe would not give.

Around the house through a side window, Randall looked into a living room. There was a white leather sofa and a recliner arranged around a large TV. The TV was on and through the screen glass showed a cartoon dog and cartoon cat. The dog hit the cat with a piece of driftwood and the cat laughed.

There was no one in the room.

Randall tried the window but it would not stutter. The pane swayed and shimmied with his fist. Overhead the sun still stung and stared.

Randall stepped back from the house. The roof had the same pattern as the stairwell, a mess of lines of scattered depth. He walked back to where the girl stood. He stood looking on inside the light. Static rattled from the transistor, nuzzled tight against her torso. He gave her a look and she shut it off. She turned around toward the house.

Randall watched as she walked toward it in the same slow path as his, up the strange steps to touch the door with both her hands, though this time the knob turned; the door opened on to the inside.

The girl looked back at Randall and closed her eyes.

The air between them wavered.

Inside, the house was cool and clean and smelled of cedar. The hardwood floors reflected their faces in the grain. They called out up the stairwell and into the adjoining rooms, peering around corners to no response, no motion. The home's air hung around them, parting.

In the short hall Randall's shoulders brushed both sides.

Upstairs they found a child's room, painted pink and draped with lace—a canopy bed piled with pillows and stuffed toys, a loom. The bed was dressed in patchwork in the same way as the girl's clothes. There were no fingerprints, no dust, no locks.

On the nightstand beside the bed there was a small picture in a frame. In it, a young man stood beside a tree with both hands behind his back.

The girl lifted the frame and stroked the glass grain with her thumb.

"My father," she said. "He looks young."

She propped the photo back on the stand to face the bed.

Across the hall they found a larger bedroom with a large oak-framed mattress and a roll-top desk stacked with new paper. The longer wall was made of bookshelves, husky spines packed end to end. Some of the books were filled with blather, math, rune symbols. The clothes inside the walk-in closet fit Randall close enough. He changed out of his sandy jean suit into blue fur pajamas and stood in the mirror trying to recognize his face.

Above the bed was an enormous painting of an ocean, slung with froth, mostly opaque.

Back downstairs, in the kitchen, they found the pantry fully stocked; the fridge overflowing with clean light. They ate peanut butter and corned beef. They ate avocado and pineapple spears, drank cold filtered water from a pitcher. As they ate, their skins began to loosen, the texture of their tanned skin and going smooth. They carried plates into the living room and ate in front of the TV where now the cartoon dog and cat were smiling and on fire. The sofas were large and comfortable and smooth. There was enough room for both of them to sit sprawled out on their own seat and sink their skins into the cushions. They watched the TV, droning. There were no news clips and no commercials.

In sleep, their warm brains drifted, slow pulses still and steady.

Randall slept with his mouth open, drooling, seeing his son was made of light, full and stitched and spotless.

The girl nuzzled a pillow and rolled over upside down and hummed.

While they lay, the house made short clicking sounds around them, slight settlings, shifts of air.

Randall woke later to the touch of something crawling in his hair. He sat up quick, with fists clenched. The girl lay across from him with the transistor. In her sleep she'd turned it on. The signal came in clearly, broadcasting the same soft-sunned song he could not place—throbbing and monotone and wordless. It sang out from the tiny, salvaged speaker from everywhere at once.

Randall blinked, his body sponging. He tried to think of where he'd been. He muttered something old beneath his breath.

The girl opened her eyes.

She smiled and watched him, her sleep still glazed and changing. She pointed past him to the window, between the thick green curtains parted wide.

Through the glass into the sand yard, Randall saw the rain there coming down—liquid rain. Plain water poured in droves. It sluiced against the paneled glass so thick he couldn't see a foot beyond. He moved to the frame and pressed his face against it, saw where below the lip the runoff had already gathered several feet. It lapped at the bottom panes, compiling upward, beaded droplets cascading down the glass.

Inside, the song continued, drawing upward, its long calm chords vibrating the air, his hair, the house.

INK

Hard to decipher in its squall—the long squirts of liquid in stretched blue pyramids descending on the yard. Soon the windows streaked so thick you could no longer trace your name. The house was full of drip: the chimney glutted; the ceiling leaking; the sinks overflowed a new pool on the carpet. What books could have been written with this excess. What squid would hide from light. Out on the back porch the level rose to lap the welcome mat. You couldn't see into the street. Everything clogged and burped and sopping. The surface reflected whatever peered into it. Overhead some sound like choking: gooed helicopters, gummy birds. The seas were heavy somewhere. I scratched my cheek and half-expected the unctuous gleam to come pouring out of me. Instead: my blood, several shades of brown. I slept what hours I could manage. I waited to wake up to something clean. In the nights, when the dripping swung low, we climbed onto the roof to try to see the city: a blubbered dot hung from the sky, a runny, rotten, murdered thing—a billion voices buried beneath, all saying the same thing over and over, smothered out.

TOUR OF THE DROWNED NEIGHBORHOOD

This is the yard where the dogs would sit by the half-wrecked shed and sweat. Dad often tied them so tight they couldn't crane their necks. Their backs flea-bit and wrecked with mange and xylophonic ribs. Moxie, Skipper, Moonbeam. Remember their howling in the hot nights when the ambulances screamed by. Remember the scummy flex of their brown backs, the lather of their sweat in suds. The year I snuck them each a sliver of my birthday cake, age 13—fudge batter, banana frosting. You should have seen those dumb dogs' eyes.

This is the driveway, cracked with gravel from the groaning of the earth. These are my initials scraped into the wet cement for which my father blacked my eye. His Corvette sat for years there dripping, no amount of wrench or sweat bringing it back to life, until finally one day the wind lifted it straight off into the air. Remember how on brown August days mom would come out and spread a towel and tan in her underwear where all could see. Her name carved in a stall of the middle school's boy's bathroom—another box now undersea.

Imagine these houses taking on water. The cold flutter of family lungs.

This is an electric chain-link fence.

This is a picture window with no picture.

This is my parents' bedroom where when they slept he'd lock the knob. The drywall damp between us not thick enough to keep a quiet. How dad would shower her in shouting. How mom would cough clods up in rip. Remember emphysema. Remember how quick the disease spread. Remember the nights I woke with nightmare and went to crawl in bed between them, finding only a door that wouldn't budge, a cold metal bauble in my hand.

Here's my room with the bunk beds I've slept in since I was seven, long after my feet hung off the end. Here's a picture of my first girlfriend, whom I never got a chance to nuzzle. This is my videotape collection. This is a butterfly knife. A conch. This is the toe nail I lost after kicking the side of the house in anger. This is a 1952 Topps Mickey Mantle rookie card in near-mint condition, just one corner burped with glitch.

This is a drawing of me on the top of a mountain waving hello or goodbye.

Imagine my innards flush with water. Imagine endless rain.

This is the chimney, where once a year we'd catch a bird. You could hear it singing through the whole house, in the attic, in my sleep. *Chirrup chirrup.* Dad would get so mad he'd stand in the hearth with a broom. He'd shriek and curse and stir up dust. If he couldn't scare the bird free, he'd start a fire. The smoke curling up its beak lines. Within an hour, the chirrup ceased. I guess the bodies stayed stuck up there somewhere, lost in charcoal smudge.

Imagine how when the water rose high enough to cover the whole house. How you could see the tip of the chimney on the lip—*an eye.*

This is the cul-de-sac where I once socked my neighbor for saying my parents were going to die. Bobby had a stye over his right eye from not sleeping—bright yellow, oozing, swollen so big he couldn't blink. He said he'd read the Bible and there was still time for absolution.

Remember how his was the first body I saw floating bloated on the rain, a school of malformed fan fish nipping at his back.

Remember how you never know it's coming until it's there and then it's there.

Imagine how they swam until their arms ached, their lungs heavy in their chest.

This is a ruined veranda.

This is where I sometimes liked to hide.

This is the mouth of the sewer. Vortex of lost balls. Remember how on hot days you could see the heat rise in wavy lines. How on that first day, after six hours of torrential downpour, the manhole overflowed and bubbled, and the water spread out from around it, washing sludge and shit into the street.

This is a makeshift graveyard where we all buried our pets. No one could say who'd started, but you could count a hundred markers: cats, dogs, ferrets, snakes, hamsters, goldfish, lizards. The dirt was soft and loamy, fat with earthworms, ripe, alive. In April the flowers grew here first. Remember when Moxie died—followed by both Moonbeam and Skipper within hours, each living off the other, connected in the pulse—my father carried them one over each shoulder. He made me watch while he struck ground, heaving. The emphysema had him too. My mother began to recite a benediction and he told her to shut her mouth.

This is blacktop concrete, great for skinning knees.

This is a children's playground.

Imagine secondary drowning where inhaled salt water foams up in the lungs.

This is a spacious 4 bed 2.5 bath colonial with formal dining area, fireplace, walkout basement, in-ground sprinklers and a kidney bean shaped pool.

This is the Anderton's, the Banks's, the Barrett's, the Butler's, the Carlyle's, the Canter's, the Crumps', the Davidson's, the Dumbleton's, the Fulton's, the Grant's, the Griggs's, the Guzman's, the Kranz's, the Lott's, the Peavey's, the Peery's, the Pendleton's, the Ray's, the Rutledge's, the Smith's, the Stutzman's, the Weidinger's, the Woods's, the Worth's.

Imagine shallow water blackout, heart attack, thermal shock, and stroke. The skies alive in color. No light, no sting, no sound.

This is street number 713, abandoned since I was eight. Murmur of murder. Phantom life. The paint was green and chipping. The grass had grown up around the hedges, the trees leafless all year round. Sometimes in the evenings you'd see a light come on upstairs. Remember the summer some kid's cousin went in during night. How he didn't come back out for hours, and later they found he'd fallen through the stairwell and snapped his back. Remember the way I sat up all hours as a preteen already balding, staring through my bedroom window at the house with one eye and then the other.

This is the last square of the sidewalk.

This is telephone wire.

This is mud.

This is a rowboat, long abandoned, rotten, mired in stagnant water.

This is the steeple, still uncovered—the high mark of the flood's thread. Remember the copper swallow of communion, the tab pressed against the tongue. Remember trying to imagine how my father could stand the burn of every evening; how his throat must have been mottled from all he'd poured through there, I imagined. How he'd seen me come home through the front door in my Sunday suit and spat.

Imagine the ocean approaching overhead. Imagine waking up under dripping ceiling. The puddle plodding on the carpet, the water already having filled mostly up the stairs. My parents' bedroom on the first floor. The coughing swallowed, calm. Remember my mother's wet head in the bedroom, a hundred thousand thin blonde protein fingers spreading out as I swam down to kiss her face.

This is a quiet evening.

This—I'm not quite sure.

Imagine nowhere. Imagine nothing. A world all swollen and asleep.

These are the tips of the tallest trees—the funny firs up to their wrecked necks, spreading out distended undersea. See the new nests brimmed with egg. The mothers' wings weak, flown for hours after food over the flat, shimmering face of endless water.

BLOOD

Though we refused to call it that—we swore not to acknowledge the innards of our fathers as they sprayed down in spectacle upon us—it woke us quickly from our visions. There was something familiar we could smell in the long glossy streams: nonstop pouring from overhead, some bottomless container. For some stretches the mesh of platelets formed sets of stairs. That week there was no sun, no moon, no dreaming, not even a word from the mouth of one neighbor or another as we waited for some end—hid and fumbling beneath only the earth's face, wide and loamy, coagulating.

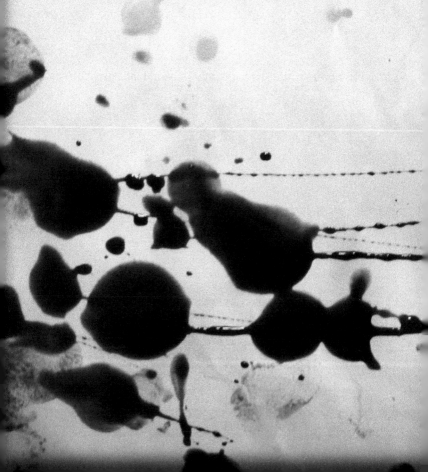

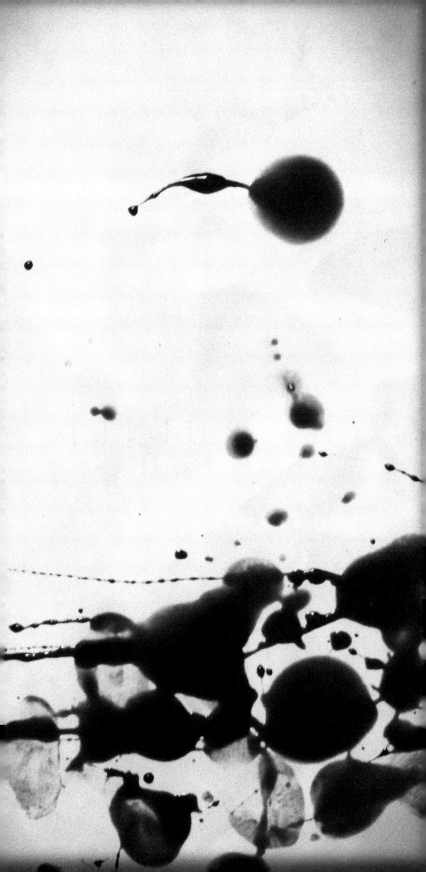

THE RUINED
CHILD

They carried the child into the outside by his wrists and ankles, wriggling. His flesh had turned translucent. His mouth would often froth. They waded waist-deep into the sewage past the upended Mustang where neighbor Bill had tried to drive—the engine crusted over now, back wheels high in the air. The rain had wrecked the city, burst the sewers, drowned the roads. Downtown was underwater. Bill, like many others, had still believed in some way out. He'd spent hours out there with a lone rope trying to yank the Mustang free, his crazed face and muscles so stretched and shining it seemed he might burst open or combust. Finally it was the dogs that had gotten to him, mange-mottled packs of ex-pets combing the old neighborhood for blood. They'd ripped him limb from limb, to rib and tendon. Gnats made short work of the remainder.

The child's first word had been *rot*. He'd been staring at his wrecked head in the mirror when he said it. He touched his reflection on the eyes. When the parents tried to take the shard away, he squealed and hugged the glass. He seemed pleased with his image, even after his body had begun to distort. Where once he'd had the father's features, his skin expunged a short white rind. First in his crevices—armpits, nostrils, teeth holes, backs of knees—then the chest and cheeks and eyes. The parents tried so much to wash the gunk away—they tried soap, peroxide, bleach, hot water, rubbing, prayer—nothing made the child clean. The thick white mush became a second skin. It smelled of burnt rubber and stung the nose.

In the evenings, the dogs threw themselves against the house. The father had been able to keep them off for several days with a shotgun until they learned he had no bullets, then they chewed through the siding on the garage and got into what little food the father had scavenged from nearby abandoned houses. The dogs wolfed down everything in seconds that the father had been determined to make last.

With the floodwaters up to their chests, the parents stopped and held the infant boy above their heads. They wore rubber gloves to prevent their own infection. In the low light the child cast no shadow.

They were looking at each other then. The father opened his mouth to say something but did not. The mother opened her mouth to say something and also didn't.

Together they held the child. They held him up until the blood moved into their shoulders and their arms began to shake. They lowered their son down slowly until they couldn't help it. They laid their son down on the muck.

The baby floated. His head sat nuzzled in the algae on the lip, awaiting strange baptism. His cackle seemed almost a language. It made the father's insides curl.

The father and the mother had been to service every Sunday for decades—until the pastor fell into spasm in midst of prayer—until the muck had lapped to cover even the steeple in its valley. All those wooden pews now underwater. All their prayers and hymns and paper money. The father remembered the taste of his dry mouth just before it filled with the copper lap of communion wine. His ass falling asleep beneath him during the sermon as he sat holding his son just so to keep the boy from screaming. He remembered the pleat of his khaki pants. Choke of his necktie. Squeak of loafer. The squelch of radio static on the drive home as his wife flipped from station to station each time a song she liked ended, searching for another amongst the noise.

The child's second word had been *nothing*. He hadn't had time yet to learn a third. The foam had begun to flake off of the carpet. He couldn't keep food inside him, couldn't see through swollen lids. The parents had gotten on their knees and begged to god to send an answer. They kissed the Bible, crossed their chests. They did not receive word.

As more time passed the child's condition worsened. The boy's hair was turning gray, then a mesh of colors. He sneezed several times a minute. He had to suck air through a tube. Things could not go on this way, the parents said to one another—their child was miserable and in pain. They felt his suffering in their stomachs, hot and dry and spreading out.

They'd come to a decision.

Among the muck the air was threaded, webbed like lettuce, grinding light. The father put his gloved hands across the child's face. He inhaled and closed his eyes.

Back at home, still braised and reeling, the parents found the front windows busted—ones they'd thought too high for dogs to enter. The living room was shredded. The dogs had eaten the innards of the mattress where the parents had slept with the baby coddled between them before his infestation. The dogs had eaten the sack of half-green leaves the father had climbed several trees for, another makeshift dinner. They'd scratched the walls and shit all over the carpet.

The mother sat in the floor limp-limbed and wept in sips of stuttered air.

The father watched her, saying nothing. Something squirmed behind his eyes. He turned from her for the attic. The attic where he kept the rope. The stairs creaked beneath him as he clambered, his raw joints cracking, the wood old and rotting, giving out.

In the far back corner there, sitting upright on a bale of insulation, the father found the child returned from where they'd left him. The child's eyes were red around the pupils, reflective in their centers. Though he no longer had the white rind, he'd swollen to twice his prior size—his head a bulbous, pulsing thing. The room stunk of rotten melon. The room seemed very small.

The mother and the father had had the child together after endless months of empty luck. The mother had suffered numerous miscarriages. They doctors said her womb was ripped, polluted. *A common problem herein* was how they termed it. The parents continued trying anyway. This was before the floods, but after the malls and movie theaters and markets had all closed. After the sky began changing color—neon pink, then white, then gold. People had been collapsing by the hundreds. The earth's face was cracking, spitting open. Hordes of grasshoppers. Gobs of bees. But then this child—their hope, their glimmer—it appeared inside her made of light. The parents were so excited they couldn't even pick a name. They spent hours on suggestions, thumbing phonebooks, testing the sound of certain syllables in their mouths, but nothing seemed quite to come together—nothing was their son.

Because no doctors' doors were open, the father performed the delivery himself. He coached the mother through her hee-hee breathing, the grunt and groan, the blather. Afterwards he couldn't flush the memory of his wife's brown blood all sputtered on his hands. There was still a spot on the carpet that stayed no matter how hard he tried to scrub it out.

The father knew this wasn't actually the child now here before him in the attic—he'd watched the bubbling go still. It was some mirage, a function of his grief. He couldn't keep himself from staring.

The ruined child opened up its runny mouth.

"One woe is past," it quoted, its voice cragged and rotten, an old man's. "And, behold, there come two woes more hereafter." Smoke rose from its speckled gums as the words came. Spittle popping on its lips.

One woe? the father thought. More like ten thousand. You could probably fit a billion woes in every day depending on how small you sliced the hour.

The child repeated: "Two woes more hereafter." It seemed to gag on its own tongue. It looked into the father, blinking. It said, "My anus is a portal."

The room around them slightly rolled.

The child's mother shouldn't see this, the father thought. He turned away and hid his eyes. He went back downstairs and locked the door behind him. He tucked a towel under the crack. Though for hours, through whatever insulation, whatever silence, the child's voice still slammed his head.

■

Back in the living room, the father found the mother staring into the staticked face of the TV. Though the programming stations had been out for months, he still caught her watching rather often, usually with her nose inches from the glass bulb, humming in tune with the sound. For a while he'd refused to let her waste the generator, but now he didn't even argue.

"Where have you been?" she asked. She didn't press him. Her hands gripped both sides of the screen. She drooled.

The father watched her for another second, then went into the kitchen and he stood there.

And he stood there. And he stood there. And he stood.

■

That night, on the carpet, nestled in half-blankets wrecked by moths, the mother spoke her want for a new child.

"Surely it was some kind of error," she said, pressed against him awkward, their limbs uncomfortable in tangle. "That first baby. That precious sorry little boy. My body needed flushing. We have to try again."

The father didn't blink. He could hardly hear her for the baby's voice still lodged on his brain. He thought of the child there in the attic just above them, pressing its large pus-smothered ear against the attic floor.

"I wouldn't try again for anything," the father said quite loudly, to make the child hear too. He did not look at the mother. "No matter what kind of light was promised. I couldn't stand it. I couldn't even."

The mother's face became a knot.

"Are you so lost already you couldn't imagine God's grace?" She touched him, her fingers icy. He couldn't look. His blood was still.

She got up out of bed.

She stood in the queer light through the doorway, seething, the gnatty skin crimped at her neck.

"If you won't help I'll find a way myself," she said.

She left the room. The father heard TV static a second later, so loud he could feel it in his teeth. The walls around him seemed to sink. He spread out with his arms and legs in her absence, stretching, the carpet warm in spots. He spoke aloud and tried to reason with her even though he knew she couldn't hear.

"God," he kept repeating.

His tongue felt fat, electric near his throat.

■

Outside, the night was runny. The father cupped air in his cheeks. He breathed and swallowed, breathed and swallowed. He lit a candle and waded back into the muck. Underneath the surface there were currents. Hard clusters near his knees. He moved to where he'd pushed the baby under, if he could remember. He reached deep in with his long arms. The muck gummed his nostrils, shook his lungs. Reaching. Reaching. Nothing. The father bit his splitting lips. He grunted, stretching harder. Hot wax dripped in slow strings down his other arm. He dropped the candle in the wet. Then the sky was nowhere. The cold face of the moon was blotted out with birthing flies.

He could not find the child.

The father called for his wife into the silence to come and guide him home by voice, but she couldn't hear or wouldn't come.

■

By the time the father made it back to the house the muck had dried across his upper half, a crust that came off in greasy chips. The stinking made him dizzy. He stripped to naked in the front yard. He tried to think of what he'd do if the dogs returned right then. He wondered if he'd fight or just stand and let them rip. He dreamed of incisors, shredding into cells.

He felt his stomach rumble. Mostly, his body had gotten used now to nothing. On worst days they'd eaten cloth or rubble.

What might the child have tasted like? he wondered.

What would the wife?

■

In the living room, still naked, mud-clung in long patterns, the father found the mother passed out with her head propped against the TV. She had a bra left on and nothing else, a see-through thing he'd long since gotten over. Normally he would have carried her to bed and tucked her in but this time he left her crooked and wet, eyes aglow.

In the morning she was still there, inch for inch. Her neck sat crumpled with the burden of her head. He moved to shake her shoulder. Gnats muddled in and around her mouth. The tongue, the meat, already rotting. She'd jabbed a kitchen knife into her stomach. Blood spread around her in an oval. Static seemed to gather at her face. The father stepped back from her, hands wet and trembling. He looked at what she'd done.

He could hear the dogs outside again, hungry, barking, bashing their bodies at the boards. The sheen of the mother's blood did not quiver in their rhythm.

Overhead he heard the baby breathing through the ceiling, smacking its gums.

Upstairs the child sat swollen even larger—now nearly five times redoubled. In its eyes the father saw translucence, the whirred white flesh of its cornea neon, raw. Its flesh was golden and covered in larvae. It was bigger even than the father.

"*The second woe is passed,*" it said, giggling and cutesy. "*And, behold, the third woe cometh quickly.*"

The father kept his face turned from the son.

"Soon your skin will rupture and your eyes will vomit grease," the child continued, his voice now several voices. "Your balls will pop and worms will wriggle and the air will liquidate. The seas will rush to smash the sky."

The breath coming off the child was spotted.

The spots, together, became light.

The father felt the thing behind his eyes spin centered, spraying.

"I don't even see you," he shouted. "You're not there."

The child guffawed. It slapped its thighs and spit up. In the spit there wriggled something. The father could not inhale. He hurried past the child and took the tools he'd long ago stored away. He left the attic again without looking. Downstairs he could still hear the child's cracked cackle even with the door closed and locked again.

He carried his wife into the backyard by the armpits. The yard was wet and sunk with residue. The trees had rotted and fallen in. Vast shapes moved on the horizon. In the dead flowerbed he found a soft spot where she could rest.

In an hour he had a hole dug.

In another hour he had her under.

Atop the mound of overturned earth, he spoke benediction: what sacred phrases he could remember. His tongue gnashed at his palate though the words were hard to taste.

■

That night the sky rained soil.

At first the father thought the sound of the pounding on the roof was the child's kick and stammer, the child's long swelling, but through the crack over the high bedroom window the father saw the great crudded gashings of loose earth coming down. The sun hung somewhere muted, disremembered of its light. He tried to think and felt his brain's wheels catching, grinding wells into his head. His extremities began to tingle, buzzed by the sudden loss of flowing blood. He felt lightheaded, zoning, dumb. He hadn't slept in several days. He sat on the wrecked mattress with his knees crossed. There was an impression left among the shredded bulges where for all those years his wife had laid, and another shaped like him. He rolled onto the ridge between their two spots and wondered how long until the ceiling gave, until the earth grew covered over. He chewed his tongue and breathed and breathed. He could hardly think of who he was. He said his name aloud so he'd remember. In repetition, each utterance grew slightly further off from what it should be.

Name, he thought. A son's name.

Son.

He sat until his head grew so heavy he couldn't hold it up.

Inside his head it was all one color. His heartbeat skittered in his throat. He did not dream.

He woke to a sour mouth some time later with someone standing over him by the bed. At first he assumed it was the child having come to smother, rub him out.

Okay, he thought. Let's go.

As his eyes grew accustomed back to the room's light, he saw the grim, loosed lines of his wife's face. She looked many years older now already. She coughed up gravel on the mattress.

"Do you remember the first time you fucked me?" she said. "How sweet your kiss was? We bought a room in an old hotel. There were flowers in my hair. I'd never met a man like you. I thought you'd take me places. Light my insides. Do you remember the way you spurted? I'd only known you ten days. You called me another name. How wise your eyes were, rolled back in your head. I had my mind on television."

She moved toward him, her body hulking. She put a leg up on the bed. He could feel the chill in her forearms, the hair there already grown out long and matted.

"Let's make this baby," she said, begging. "A new life. Please, my dearest. Squirt me up."

He pushed her off. He got up and moved out of the bedroom and slammed the door shut behind him. He waited for her to pound or push but there was nothing. There was no tick, no garbled gobbling. The house was still.

The father opened the door and saw just a room. A room he'd lived and slept in for many years.

Through the window, instead of dirt now, the sky was pouring roach. The critters hit the earth and wriggled upright, already a foot high off the soil. Other bugs erupted from a new budding crevice—leeches, gnats, mosquitoes, wasps. He could hear the collective hum of wings and cilia vibrating in the air.

The dogs were at the front door. They smashed themselves against the frame, howling, hungry, chewing each other. They'll be inside soon, the father thought. His stomach gurgled. His brain began to click. There were things that he might have known once. Places he had been. Days and numbers, thoughts, corruptions, wishing, exits, lists, and vows. Everything seemed to wriggle in his shoulders. He spoke a thing he knew aloud—it came out wrong.

Upstairs, he found the child again. It had swollen through the attic. Its body pressed against the roof, warping the beams. Its huge bright red pupils spun for focus. The father recognized in the child's face, even so bloated, certain of the mother's features, and his own. This thing they'd made together.

The father wanted to kiss the ruined child's dappled lips. He wanted to climb inside its size and live forever.

The child was saying something. Its voice had also grown enormous, even larger than the house. The child's tenor seemed to scratch the room, to turn the very air to liquid dust. The child's voice echoed in the father's head—a self inside himself incanting with each the word the son then said. At first the words seemed, to the father, nothing, nonsense, a voice thrumming through his skin to rip it, though with all of these words coming out now, the father began to feel something soft inside him glisten. His body washed, an old tide rolling.

All these words, the father felt, were words he knew he wanted—these words were written in his flesh and on his flesh and all around it, in the dirt and water, on the air.

And now the massive baby lay before him, coocooing, while outside the earth began to writhe.

And now the father opened up his numbing mouth and gave his son a name.

MANURE

I will not speak of this day.

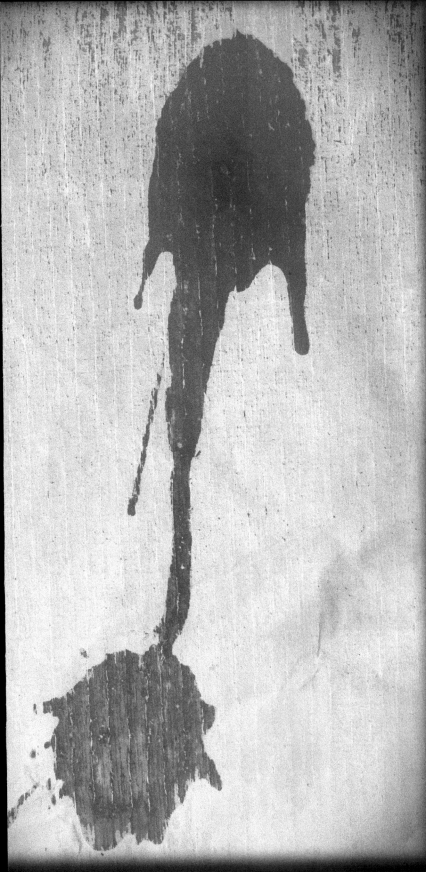

BATH
or
MUD
or
RECLAMATION
or
WAY IN / WAY OUT

When the final crudded current first burst somewhere off the new coast of Oklahoma, I was seventeen and cross-eyed. The storm spread in a curtain. It came and cracked the crust that'd formed over the fields, the junk that'd moored up in our harbors. It washed away most everything not tied down and most everything that was. All those reams of ugly water. All that riddled from the sky.

My family huddled hidden under one another in the house our Dad had built alone. The house where we'd spent these years together. The old roof groaned under the pouring. The leaking basement filled with goo.

LOST: my gun collection.

LOST: every board game you can think of.

LOST: mother's bowling trophies (30+).

LOST: our hope for some new day.

For weeks after the onslaught, I spent each afternoon up to my knees, shoveling mud from off of what remained of our crushed huddle. The sun had come back black, redoubled. What hadn't sunk or gone to mush now sat neck-deep, blobbed and burbling. The earth was bottomless and greedy. It promised to swallow whatever stayed out long enough to glisten. Me and my brothers, though; we fought hard. It was the twelve of us, blonde and hungry, each often nipples-deep and digging through the night. In the mornings, in the dew light, with the sun so hot it singed our hair, the gunk would form a crust—then we could take turns together sleeping, though you could never fully close your eyes. The mud might shift or moan. I'd seen trees get sucked in suddenly like spaghetti into lips. Sometimes, in my basement bedroom, you could hear the screaming through the soil—the folks from other homes who couldn't fight the heave. I'd watched the Johnsons go down treading, their old muscles ripped and overheating. Mrs. Johnson's bright yellow noggin with curled hair ribbon bobbed on the surface a full day before it sunk.

It wasn't long before we fell too. One by one, I watched my brothers fizzle. Eleven boys, aged eight to eighteen, each so tired their pupils spun. You couldn't do much once it had you—the mud held tight and suckled quickly. I watched with sore hands as each one tuckered, went under deep, their small heads gone.

At night I drummed up stories for our mother in her linens, so fat she couldn't fit out from the house. Her gut had swelled to fill the bedroom mostly; the ocean swelled inside her too. She ate in misery. I didn't blame her. She'd lost the most of all of us. I sold excuses for each drowned baby: *Derry's gone to Grandma's, Momma. Phillip's run off with a girl.* She watched unblinking as I went on. She hadn't spoke up clear in years. She sometimes croaked or cracked or gobbled, or sputtered gibberish, glassy-eyed: YHIKE DUM LOOZY FA FA, she said. ZEERZIT ITZ BLENN NOIKI FAHCH.

I knew she could still hear me. She felt my voice inside her head.

We remaining went on working even knowing how the mud would never stop. In certain seconds we even maybe believed we could beat it, live forever. Soon, though, even Georgie grew too tired. I kissed his forehead, just above the mud lip. Shortly after we lost Bill. Then Thomas. Freddy. Dennis. After Phillip faltered, there were no longer enough arms to hold the house. The windows popped and bubbled. The roofing puckered. The concrete turned to slick. The mud caked and swallowed over. Then there was nothing left but dark. I prayed Mother would forgive me. I could hear her just below the surface. Her together with the brothers. Then, soon enough, there was silence.

Our home's foundation sat gashed and flat.

With no more brothers, nothing nowhere, I closed my eyes and waited, last of all of us, alone. I prepared to take my place, forthcoming. I lay in the mud and breathed and waited. I prayed my brain would shut off lightly, without aching, without sting— that when I opened my eyes under all that deep mud, I'd see all my brothers' faces stretched with grins.

Instead, that night I watched the moon rise. I rolled and slathered, squealing. I pushed my arms in up to my elbows. The mud stayed firm, an evil bed. The earth didn't want me. I screamed and nattered at it. I pleaded and I praised. I begged for it to open up. Overhead the moon burned through the ruining sky. I thought of heavy things, of ripping. I pressed for soft spots in the stink. I searched and cursed and, hungry, prayed. I let crap gather in my eyes.

Some sprawl later, still alone above ground, I got up and went to walk. I moved with nowhere settled in me. It was mostly cold out, despite the burning. My exposed skin gushed bright from the sick sun.

I thought about the week my family camped at the shore during the red tide with dead fish slushing up in piles. My father stood among the flipless bodies and picked the ones that had yet to go soft. We ate with our fingers and our mother sung and the ocean gurgled at the sky—like there was something living in it. Afterwards, with Mom still singing, we buried papa neck-deep in the sand. His gobby cheeks puckered and sand-dusted, as were his lashes, his thinning hair. He claimed to feel things moving near his knees. "They're biting," he said in smile. Years later, we buried him on that same shore, wreathed in crimped seaweed—*as I thought this thought for the last time, I felt it leave me and a new void birthed in my mind*—

I soon came to other places. The face of the earth sat spread like rotting mayonnaise. Such cities sunk under the surface. Ones I'd never see again:

LOST: our middle school.

LOST: the bowling alley.

LOST: the shopping mall where I'd been born.

In some places the shit was stacked so high you could not see where it stopped. Elsewhere, the divots broiled for miles. The mud had many colors. Mounds of blue; green slicks of lichens; gray gobs and puddled ruin in brown and pink and tan. In orange and gray and yellow. It stretched forever. Certain places spread translucent. Underneath you could see kids enfolded, their faces hopeful, their bodies swollen and distended.

I'd never been in love.

Over the hills then, my sore feet rumbling, not sure when or how or what—what was wanted with all this terror, this slippage, gunk and froth. What these people in these buried buildings had done—or not quite done. I thought of my brothers, each forever under, though now the more I thought the harder it was to remember. Suddenly I couldn't image even Richard, with whom for years I'd shared a bed. Our backs kinked on the mattress. His night-breath in my face. I squeezed my forehead to form some shape beneath it. My little brothers, all of us in father's likeness, a set of dolls, each slightly smaller.

Soon my stomach's grinding took over all. I followed the sound in lure—my hum suspended in the sky, an atlas. My knees were hung with strings of leeches. *Suck*, I thought, *suck me empty. Draw me out and lay me down.* I couldn't think of what good my blood had done me. They should have it, they should see.

See me coming through the black fold with my hair all fat in knots.

See my skin striped several colors like the mud.

Colors. I knew such colors. That was mostly all I knew. They ate through my vision in clustered patches. All around, as in my memory, the plots of color grew and flew in glittered flakes.

In the colors, I held no yearning.

In the colors, I met a child.

I met a child who told me to keep walking. She had a faultless face and straight dark hair. She had eyes that spread all through me. She seemed like someone I had known. Or would know. Or could need nearer. She reached in color and touched me on the neck. She said if I kept walking there would be a reason. There would be windows. Some kind of something. I had to trust, she said, to get anywhere. Not all of her language I could understand.

I said for her I would go on.

I would go on, at least, until I found a way to join my brothers.

My brothers, there'd been eight of them. Eight or seventeen or eighty. Some multiple of three.

My brothers, they were good boys. They'd been…

I knew…

I couldn't feel my face.

See the drowned field where once I'd thrown a wild pitch and knocked a kid between the eyes. He was never quite the same. He roamed the neighborhood undressed and eyes closed. He knew everyone by feel. He could feel your face and name you and then he'd laugh and laugh and laugh.

That boy, his name was…

We… I'd…

See the rind of trees all crumpled. Combed to one side like the white hair of my father in his last days. Out in front of our house in shorts and dress shirt, a huge crucifix around his neck. Shouting in my mother's crippled language: what was coming, what would be.

My father's name's…Troy. No, Tony. Robert.

Robert's my name. I think.

Shit.

See my veins vibrating in their choked skin.

See my brow meshed in lines of unknown light.

See the caved-in parking deck where for several weeks the newly homeless flocked. Once in this deck, people left their cars and shopped for Christmas. The sound of its collapse that Sunday evening shook us even far away. Now that was over. All that was gone. I felt that sound, though, curled in my stomach, crudding over, washing out. I felt it replicate all through me. It brought cohesion in the color.

The cohesion formed a lantern.

The lantern lit a path.

I walked the path with brain wide open, thinking through each thing I thought I knew one final time.

■

Up the yards then. Through the bogged lots. The fronts of houses stunned or smushed. The cob of old mud dried to figures, streams of dead beds in the earth. And the lost lamps. And the smeared hills. The sewers overflowed. Here and there, perhaps, a flower, its sad head puckered through the muck. The blacktop parking lots and cul-de-sac'd streets where once we'd thrown dice or chucked a ball—all so cracked now, rumbled wrong. There was something in the air in gloaming, a blistered chill even in the heat.

I walked across the roofs of many houses. The sun unblinking, on and overhead through evening into night. I knew night now by the stutter of warped insect critters crowing. They sung together, awaiting nowhere.

OK now, I thought. *OK.* I thought: *I am going somewhere. Somehow I will summer. I will find food and return. I will pluck sausage sandwiches from some strange tree and carry them back to feed my loved. My how? My who? My brothers.* I kept saying it aloud: *Brothers*—those guys with eyes the same as mine. I felt them watching me from somewhere. They were waiting. All was fine.

Through the pasture bright with blue mud, cracked so sharp in turrets, dry with tremor. Spores shorn endless in the raw light, spreading out in webs of gray, green, gold. I felt a small pop in my sock and started bleeding. The veins inside me screaming blue, red, brown.

Colors, colors. I thought to call the girl. She had not given me her name. I tried old names I'd once used for others: Freda, Franny,

Fawn, and Farrah. I could not remember who they were now, though the words enlivened, short wires in my brain, leading nowhere, sparking out. I wanted to touch them. I wanted something.

Instead, ahead, I saw a cow. It stood blinking under an overpass, its enormous head cocked to watch me come. In its mottled side skin, I saw a face splotched. I saw someone opening their mouth. Inside the mouth, I heard my brothers screaming. I felt their tendons sizzle in me. I felt the nights we'd all slept knee to knee in the same room in that slow-sinking house—our mother on the floor beneath us, her body quaking, waiting for something to click or come undone. We were old boys in those small bodies. We'd come into the world each already stung. I felt their buzzing in me rupture, bubble.

I heard the cow say, in mom's voice: YO VOT IXHT VOD SIBBUM KLIMMITCH.

Mom. Mom's voice. I felt her.

I looked again.

Overhead the sky was melting, the cracked cream color rubbing off in cogs of brine. The fields far ahead around me in endless pudding, studded here and there with what had been: homes and houses, hair and heirlooms, habits, hallways, hauntings, hope.

■

Other shit began to happen. Behind the sky, I saw _____. The clips of drips of dropping muddle, scratching the face of everything in long bolts as flat as the back of my hand. And zapped in groggy columns things were melting out of nowhere, big rungs of hung gob spurting from sections overhead. And the skewed lobs of architecture and landscape bowled in rhythms clogged with problems, no repetition. I could hardly stick a foot straight; I was, like, wobbly hobbling through the dead grass. There was everywhere to walk now. Everywhere and none at all. I could feel my fiber peeling—my blood spread thin—my pupils slurred.

There couldn't be much time. Time, the ship, the shit, the sentence. The earth still refused to suck me under. No, not so easy, not like that, it promised. It wanted to test and tempt and make me beg, and even then just _____ inside me. I had a vision of the girl above, then to my left and to my right, each one silent and gorgeous, stringing me alone, to here or there. I no longer believed that I had something—that there would be better—that we could nuzzle. I just wanted the air to fill inside me and compress and spread out and tickle the way it seemed to inside her. The way she winked and blinked in the _____ space I felt if I jumped right I might glide straight through, but each time I gathered the ignition, then she'd shift, she'd sweat around me.

I lunged angry, blind, corroding. I swatted at the sky.

I ran and chased her straight into that blob of nothing, into a leaning where all was still.

Here the earth lay flat and long and unrunny. I felt my thighs, now burning from output, suddenly solid and ready, standing on true dirt. A circle of clean trees appeared before me. I blinked and blinked.

Into the trees I trotted meanly, keeping them fixed center in my brain, fearing they would disappear again, some prolonged jinx.

Among the trees, though, in the center, the small girl sat on tufted grass. Her flesh pale as nothing. Her hair in steam and bright gown gleaming. I couldn't see to see her eyes, though, so glowing they burned my teeth. I could only look just off to one side. Overhead—the sky still scrunched and overrun. In my coal stomach—her lone voice.

Where are your brothers? she said, knowing.

What brothers?

The ones you had.

I had brothers?

You did.

She watched, silent, while I tried to remember. She looked sad.

Dig, she said.

She seemed to hover off the ground.

Dig, she said again.

I didn't have a shovel and I told her. Such things we'd all long lost, though now I couldn't think of what. My brain wormed in want of recognition, turning over and over in cold sputter.

She shook her head.

She spoke a language.

Some feeling brought me to my knees.

With fingernails shorn and mud-clung, I scratched into the earth. I felt so numb I couldn't stutter. Something buzzed behind my eyes. I ripped the grass away in handfuls. The gravel made me bleed.

Under the first surface, there was loam: sand, silt, humus, and manure. I slung it, reeling. I dug further. My forehead pounded in my gut. The girl stood above me, looking over. She whispered little things. She pressed a thumbprint into my neck flesh. I dug through deeper layers, heaving the earth. My arms ached with the yearning.

The earth changed colors every inch: from one bright red bed where the earthworms had stopped wriggling; to the grayish murk of deadened roots; to the gray-blue glisten of long-hidden soil uncovered; then into the harder crusting, where the soil slipped from brown to heavy black, so thick and enriched I could hardly pry.

Then, there, hung in the deepest mud, I heard my brothers singing from below. Set in the gunk, the spackled crack of it, I heard a melody I knew I knew. It was a hymn Mom had once sung to each of us when we were young enough for her to knead. They were in there, them, my brothers, whose names I could now recite in order, packed in clay: Derry, Bill and Georgie (twins), Thomas, Freddy, Dennis, Phillip, Joseph, Richard, Sumner, Murphy, Jim.

And somewhere deeper, snug below them, I knew, my mother—Ann—her bad back creaking with the bruised spin of the earth.

And deeper still, perhaps, my father—David—that soft old man with whom I'd never had a final word.

I dug quicker now, something in me unsealing, seething, swum in the pummel of my blood.

FLESH

For one long hour that red morning: gristle, cartilage, tissue, tendon, vein, and bone. Some would try to gnaw the gray meat. Some would choke with fistfuls in their cheeks. Others knew better from the stinking. The bubble of the sky. I'd already burned what I remembered. I didn't search long for their names: the heads and necks and cheeks of all these raining someones someone once had likely loved.

WATER
DAMAGED
PHOTOS
OF OUR
HOME
BEFORE
I LEFT IT

(1) A framed print of our family dressed in Sunday best—my father wears a bolo tie; my mother's hair is teased. Our skin is tanned, unstretched and peachy, except for Tommy, who seems fevered. We're all looking just off to the right; wide-eyed, brimmed, unblinking, hypnotized by something just out of the frame.

—The glass over this photo, slightly cracked, has allowed small splotches in, leaving beads of spreading moisture to warp us polka-dotted, pepper-fired.

(2) The plum tree in our front yard the morning after it was struck three times by lightning. The branches are scorched and scraggly, amputated, the trunk split right down the middle. I'd watched the conflagration from my bedroom window—Mom refused to let me on the porch. I could feel the heat kiss through the panes. The tree burned beneath a crumpled sky. By the time the men had doused the fire the entire yard was mostly black.

—Here only the handwritten caption has gone runny, my mother's handwriting washed illegible.

(3) Tommy on his ninth birthday in the bottom bunk. His cheeks are puffed and ruddy. His lids are swollen shut. I am sitting on the ground beside him trying to coax a smile. I'd helped unwrap his only present—a toy shotgun, long as he was. He kept staring down the barrel. Later that same evening we'd find him still clenching it against his bright blue forehead with gnats already in his ears.

—This photo appears to have been crumpled before even the water: someone had hated to have to see. Major warping near the middle obscures Tommy's chin and lips, though if I had to guess I'd say he's smiling. I cut my head out of the photo with a pair of pinking shears.

(4) *The neighbors' dog with hair grown out so long he can hardly walk. His pupils shine deep inside the matting. The neighbors nowhere and not returning. My mother refused to let me bring him food: even trash scraps he could have choked down. He was starving. In the night the dog would scream. Soon dogs swarmed around in droves—entire packs with hair that dragged behind them, caught on trees. Their shedding clogged the gutters. The streets would quickly fill.*

—The photo paper is ruffled, crackling—the sound of it stings my teeth.

(5) *A wide shot of the fence my father built before his exit. He needed something to occupy the days after having been let go from the electric plant—my brother's sickness had spread into him as well. Each day he worked from before dawn well on into dusk until he couldn't see his hands. The wall was made of stone and stood higher than the house. You couldn't see anything beyond it. If it hadn't been for Mother's nagging, he wouldn't have bothered to leave a gate. When he was finished, he sat in the evenings on a stool an arm's length from the wall, staring head on right into it, waiting for it to speak.*

—A mold has formed on this one, small splotches of off-green, spores that blister into faint rings spiraled, a cosmos-shaped mosaic of bacteria.

(6) *My father curled in my mother's lap, her face obscured by paper mask. Behind the camera I wore one also, my breath enclosed around my face. We'd made the masks after the news reports of whole hotels full of people collapsing overnight. Planes falling from the air. Light bulbs and TVs bursting. Dad looks so small in mother's arms. His hair's down to his ass. Her eyes are shut. His eyes are open—the light blue splintered black, the skin around his lashes puckered, moist. The masks had come too late.*

—The insects got to this one quicker—the paper is eaten through and through.

(7) *The attic, stocked with Father's things, packed in unlabeled cardboard boxes. Stacked up so high on top of one another there's no room to move. In the upper left-hand corner, a hive is being built.*

—The whole photo blanched a slight shade browner, as if viewed through beer bottle glass.

(8) Several copies of the same image: me in a corduroy shirt, hair mussed, not smiling, the last school photo me or anyone in the neighborhood would pose for before the walls were buried underwater. Before the whole city began swelling. Before trees fell on the house. In my eyes the ricochet of such a short flash—the zapped gunk running of my pupils, my clenched teeth.

—Each copy of me offers a slight variety of spoil—some so warped you can't even read me—some where there is nothing left to hold.

(9) The backyard covered end to end with pupal casings.

(10) The concrete cul-de-sac cracked wide open.

(11) An overexposed image of the sky swelled purple and maroon, taken a few hours before it started with such raining, bringing the very wet that ruined these pictures.

—These three are all primarily intact.

(12) *

—This one's so destroyed I can't tell what it might have been.

(13) Mother, shaggy headed, sober, standing in the stairwell to the attic, her soft cheeks flaked brown and teeth loosed like Tommy's had, holding a hammer against her bloated stomach, staring straight on into the camera to shatter the lens with both her eyes.

—The edges of this photo are mush—the paper so runned and crummy it comes off on my fingers.

(14) The front door in the kitchen, boarded over—my sore, banged thumb half-obscuring the lens. Not visible in the photo is everything that door held out, the endless scratching, gnashing, drone.

—This photo is stuck to the front of another that won't pull off without ruining. In the loose corner of the covered photo are striated reams of light.

(15) The hole in our roof, taken from my mother's bed where I laid for hours trying to breathe her sickness in. Hating my skin for not getting paler. My teeth for not rotting out. Wondering why I would have to be the one to hold the camera. Beyond the roof, the sky scratched black in the middle of the day. And Mother still beside me, her face grown over, fingers knotted.

—Pasty, smudged and crumbling, buggy, marred: even the ruin is ruined.

(16) My mother as a young girl, blonde, holding a blue balloon larger than her torso; her grin so real it looks inhuman, her lips stretched and eyes ignited. In the air around her a kind of haze, a glow, a swelling that has nothing to do with weather.

—This one is clean, if rumpled, from all these days I've kept it clutched and slept with it pressed against my forehead; endless minutes trying to pry her from the paper, to make her flat lips whisper clearer what to smother, where to grow.

GLITTER

The sky alive and brimming, worse than the prior dust had been—geese like disco balls; magic breathing; the sun a holograph on the horizon—some great celebration overhead to which we had not and would not be invited. The glitter came through the punctured roof and stuck in our hair, our moist wounds, our running eyes. I couldn't even think to see regardless. I sat nowhere and let it drench me. I licked my arms to taste the shimmer.

EXPONENTIAL

The wall stood on the morning. Through the window I could not see. A huge flat black on the horizon. I'd slept until my belly woke me gnawing. *I'd learn to call it Brother.* I got out of bed and made my way through the webbing I'd hung to keep the nits off. Not that I slept. Not that I ever, or even wanted, as when I did I held visions: not of what was coming, but what had already been. The screaming of my father as they dragged him down the stairs. *Who ever wants to hear their father bawling? My mom had gone in hush.* I slunk into the hallway where water'd warped the walls, the paisley paper run to mush. Mold had spread over our family portrait. The overhead lamp lay flush with eggs that hid the light. I'd wrapped my head in gauze. I'd used the same strip for several months, until the cloth turned brown over my mouth from the steady stream of gunk and rheum. *Now it was inside us. Tickling my dreamhead. A bit more of me each day.* Outside the porch sat rotten, lapped by the lake swoll to an ocean. So many days I'd sat on sand and watched my little brothers splash, and dad had flushed our dinner from that small bog until the fish grew so large he couldn't reel them. And then the rain; and then the swelling—the pond's circumference tripled, quadded. Soon you couldn't see one end from the other, there where we'd once been baptized, Marco Polo'd. It grew to lap the house. *One night a cod blipped at my window, his scummy eyes unblinking, a mnemonic whisper through the glass: What will one day come will come and find us, you and I and I and you goodnight.*

■

Now near the middle of the dead tide the wall divided the wrecked sky—monolithic, blue and edgeless, stretching forever out at both ends and upwards into wherever. The sun still sat on our side, blinking in and out under erupted clouds, but the other half of everything—where the mall'd been, where my grandmother drowned with her reams of hair, where so many nights alone now I'd watched the moon try still to gleam—gone. Even from my distance I saw splotches where birds had flown into the flat surface. Below their bodies floated. *Such things I'd fished up since the stilling: copper bottles, bits* of head, even once a violin—some nights I sat and tried to play the songs I could remember. The wall absorbed all sound. Even in mid-afternoon, when on most days you could hear the buzzing from far off—the shouting men, creak of machines—the silence hurt my mind. The water was colder than I remembered. Its new grip blipped my blood. I'd come to wash my face the day before, to clean away the dust that wore the air. Heat had mowed the fields dry, had withered my first brother. His pink skin grown tight like old tobacco. The second brother starved. As of now I weighed eighty pounds, at least by my best guess in the mirror; its silvered surface cracked down the middle. I was good at not eating. I'd stayed thin even when each night we all sat down together. In want of ending up one day on glossy paper, my skin forever memorized. The wall seemed to watch me now with one enormous lidless eye. I went inside and shut the door and turned around and turned the lock—I hadn't in forever; what to hide from?; who would come? Down the hall then, to my bedroom, that door closed also, that lock keyed, through the webbing with my back turned, back to bed among the wet to weep.

■

The wall was still there in the evening and the next morning into noon. I felt it even with the windows covered; with my head hid beneath the bed. It seemed projected in my pelvis—one more disruption in my flesh. So long without eating had made me mushy, my organs on display through sickly skin. I could hear it whisper to me, mostly nonsense, ingrained in brain in lines of Braille: SLIBBITZ NOESSDUM VIKUD KLIMMER, OHST IFTS BEED BOD YAKCLISSO OYT VU EIEE. It refused to quiet during sleeping; often even louder, aimed. The words vibrated my vertebrae. My stomach curled and bubbled. Sometimes I'd get stuck on the ground. I spent several days dizzy like that, my insides runny, upside-down. I tried to remember the way my father focused during those weeks of losing hair. How despite the fact his teeth went loose and his eyes stung and he lost his nails and strips of skin, he still sat up and tried to listen and kissed our faces for goodnight. I clung to live in each every inch of him. Of what we'd had. Of where I'd been. No one would say where he'd been taken. When I gave his name aloud they said Who? The wall's words got louder. I could taste them. I could read them in my teeth. They overran all other. They wanted my attention. In slow increments I learned the rhythm. I held the syllables in my cerebrum until with study they formed sense: COME TO ME. COME TO ME SOON. COME IN HERE. COME. COME. I punched my head, refused to listen. I tied myself down to the bed. I tried to speak over the interruption but my words became another echo: COME NOW. BRING THE GIFT. I touched the window. I could see it. It was waiting. I could see.

■

After they'd taken my mom and father I'd tried to be a mother to those boys. I'd tried to establish something, to brush all thoughts of hell out from their minds. In the evenings, when the skies fell, when the water beat the brick, it was so hard not to shake. I coached them with unsure words. I tried to move the way our mom had. I tried to speak in her sweet voice. I couldn't do it. I knew beforehand. I saw it in my sleep. *If they hadn't crumbled on their own I would have left them another way.* On the porch I'd lashed a tin tub with ribbon to girder in case of need for quick escape—i.e. crumbling, i.e. disease, i.e. some unclean presence like this wall. I stepped in with both feet, buoyant, bumbling, my small frame barely making the basin bob. I took the soup spoon—the same my mother had turned our broth with, spanked our butts—and dipped it into the liquid, birthing a short ripple on the lip. A breed of mosquitoes zipped and clustered. One burrowed in my ear. *Where they got their blood these days I couldn't figure. I'd once cut myself and felt no drip.* I pulled my mother's dress over my muzzle and stirred the basin outward. Over my shoulder my porch grew smaller. The trees hung waterlogged and bending, hugging around me in bouquet. I floated through them with each grunting stroke until I felt a current and slid in. The water hadn't moved in months. I'd seen faces in the film. Now I seemed to spur on toward the high wall, sucked in by magic, magnet. The lake had spread more wide than I'd imagined. The tip of the capitol building's gold dome, several miles off, glinted in recognition, drowning. Hardly half of the high cathedral sat above the water. I thought of Grandma, of her hovel. Her brittle body sandwiched under leagues, nipped and bloated six times her size. *Perhaps I should be so lucky.* Further out the air sunk cooler. My breath began to plume. The metal basin stuck to my feet and fingers, frost etched on my face. It was getting dark. Hard to tell if temporary or the beginning of the night—the sun would lose itself so often, light might shine five minutes and be gone for weeks. My stomach somersaulted. I bumped through a layer of dead geese. I felt a panic rumbling; my stomach itched full of mice. Coming closer I could see the wall was less blue than black and made of perfect polished stone. It had symbols of some strange language writ embedded. The more I looked they became numbers. The more I looked they became names—once I knew I knew by syllable but couldn't connect to any eyes. *So many gone. Had I forgotten? Already lost inside me deep?* As I thought each word it appeared before me, somehow transcribed on the surface, slightly off: SO MANY GONE. YOU'LL HAVE FORGOTTEN. LOST INSIDE YOU. DEEP. Overhead the face of the wall stretched forever. It cut the cold, a clean protection. I spread both hands flat against it. My fingers tingled in the heat. Felt something open in me, ringing—a wound wide as the sky.

■

Back at home, locked in my bedroom, my stomach began to swell. At first the water simply pooching, then bobbing outward, more rotund. The grinding turned to stretching. My abdomen ballooned. I wiggled with the heft of it, learning to negotiate the rooms. *What rooms were left now, anyhow—the kitchen was ceiling-high with crap; the den buried in some kind of fluid; the basement full of worms.* Soon I couldn't stand. My gut weighed twice as much as me. I spread-eagled on the floor. I stuck sewing needles in my belly button. I begged god to make it end. In the mirror my face was licked with burns and incisions that formed another face, one the wall had drawn. Three hours later my baby brother came out screaming in a flood of sludge. My father's spitting image—full blonde hair, mustache and teeth. For days after I could feel the bleeding, the scumming over, the slow seal. So long the house had sat dead silent and now it swam with squeal. The baby babbled at all hours. He had the same voice as the wall, all gob. He got tangled in my webbing and refused to let me help him loose. When I tried to touch him, he'd cringe and wriggle. He came to the foot of the bed and bit my feet. We spent several days like that, at odd ends, learning where and who and how. He did not need me to teach him. On his second day he was toddling around the room. On his third he spoke the language of the wall. He said: EICHJUN LIBBVUT PEM. PIZZIT SVIMMY-NARGER IEH UNT SNAH. He collected nits and sucked their fluid. I couldn't make him stop. His small eyes seemed to want to puncture. If I played dead, he'd pet my face and kiss my ears—when I opened my eyes he went away. Still I couldn't help but feel some great swelling for him, in a place I'd once felt something else. Outside the wall was growing. Its size displaced the water. It lapped the window higher every hour. I prayed aloud for the cod, but it did not come. Sediment ground our house's frame. I thought of my grandmother elsewhere, already finished. Grandmother—I could not recall her name. I could not recall the lines of her face on those days when she'd held me—days when she'd—when she'd—what? On the bed my backbone tensed trying to remember. I stretched into my mind and felt nothing. No small indenture of where I'd come from. In my memory, where even moments earlier my father's face had sat, I felt nothing but flat black blank. *Just the wall.* It was growing. I could hear it. It was forcing water through the window seams. Divots had opened in the ceiling. The pressure shook the walls. I grabbed the child and moved into the hall. It was raining there. The carpet sloshed thick at my feet. I climbed the stairs up to the attic where for years we'd stored our photo albums, birthday letters, Christmas ornaments, baby blankets. The worms had eaten through them. I put the remnants to my face and sniffed, after something clean inside. I dragged the moth-holed blanket, now a napkin, across my brother's head to keep it dry. I could feel the wall expanding in my chest now. I could feel it want me at the window. At the small pane I rubbed the glass till I could see. The wall had reached the front yard, still moving, becoming huge, becoming all. This wall of nothing. This smudge of black. *My strum, my love, my humble.* My brother squeamed in my lap beneath me. He screamed for recognition. He didn't have a name yet. I would give him mine, so I could remember. My name. My name. The wall was buzzing. My name I hadn't heard aloud in years. *Was it even mine now? Would I want it if it was?* My brother spoke: YOU HAVE A NEW NAME. YOU WILL WANT IT. YOUR NAME IS AKVUNDTBLASSEN. YOUR NAME IS XICTYHIAY BLODDUM YAHF. YOU ARE HERE. THE NAME IS MINE. As he spoke, the wall spoke with him, becoming one voice, pronged together. I found myself echoed aloud and repeating, spreading my new name into my head. I drooled. My head was bright warm. I couldn't feel my legs. I covered my lips with one hand, humming. I put my other thumb in Brother's mouth. While he bit the blood out of my soft skin, I turned to the window and pressed my forehead flat and prayed into my palm.

))))))))))))))))))))))))))O)))))))))))))))))))))))))))))))))))))))
)))))))))))))))))(((((O)))))(((
(((((((((O)))
)))))((O)))))))
)))))))))))))))))))))))))))))))((((((((((O)))))))))))))))))))))))))))(o)
OO((O))))))))))
)))(
((o)))))))))))O((((((
((((((((((((((((((((((((((((((((((O))))))))))))))))))))))))))))))))
))
((((((((((((We were there then, me and Brother.)))))))))))))))
(OOOO((((((((((((((((((((O)))))   ))))))))))))((((((((((((((((((((((
((O)))))))))))))(((((((
(((((((((((((O))))))))))))))))))))))))))O))))))))((((((((((((((((((((
(((((((O))))))))))))))))))))))(((((O)))))))))))))))))))))))))
))(((o(((((o(((o))())
((((((((((((((((((((((((We were there then.)))))))(
)))
)))))))))))))))))))))))))))))((((((((OO(((((((((((((O)))))))))
(((((((((O)))))))))O)OO((
((((((((((((((((((((((((((O))O)))))))))))))))))))(((((((O)))))))))))
((((((((((OO))))((O)))
(((O))(((OOO(OO((((((((((((((((OOOO))((((((((((We were. (())
))O)))))(O(o)OOO))(((O)))))))))(O))))))))))))))))))))))))
)))))))))))))))))))))))))))))))))))((((O))O(O)))))))))))))))
((O)))))))(((((((((((((((((OOOOO(((O)(OO(((O)(o))O(((((We were.

LIGHT

What where would function in such luster? I'd nearly given up. There were voices in the muck somewhere, but none that I could need. Our roof laid miles beneath now, no doubt, you couldn't see up or on or out beyond the window. You couldn't hear a shudder in the grease shifts, in the unlidded clap of utter. It came at once, not some intrusion, but a bouquet opened over all. The light spread through the layers laid already. It drank the water; lit the dust; it curled ants and aphids up to nothing; it refracted through the glass of our gone rooms; split a billion ways reflected off the sheen of teeth; ripped through the glitter and the clots of blood and meat and shit in streams of staticked color—colors in eons, color gloaming, one hue for every inch we'd leaked. It burst at the center of somewhere I had not been forever—spread without motion, spread and spreading. Its skin so bright you couldn't see it. Its knees so sharp you couldn't walk. The house came open. The yard was not there. The street was not there. There was light. The light rained down. It came down on us. It came in all through and through.

BLOOM ATLAS

SURFACE(S)

—Would the slick sock of the ocean please consume me and not remember? Up here the sog goes on forever. Shopping malls and shooting ranges and apartment buildings deep beneath. A wronged froth foaming over our years together, awaiting evaporation under human sky. Now ripped to ribbons. Backyards buried. Our mottled sun. The crumbs we called plantations. Cemeteries weathered to no headstone. All my brothers and their women and their children's children unmarked and eye to eye. The ocean's face: a thick lick of grime and white rice and spit and petrol and old blood. Somehow I am up here. Somehow I am unsplit. Throat ripped in undone cattle. Skin tanned so thick I'll never feel.

DIVE

—I crack the crust open with my forehead. The water slaps my chest, succumbs me under. Sludge slick through my hair. Grit gummed up in my nostrils. Cold metal in my brain. With the slow sling of my blubbered arms I stroke along the lip. The wet so warm it's close to breathing as on long August Georgia nights. Scum of green and lipids brimming, algae afghans worn on dead waves. I swear some of this pulp has vision, heartbeat, teeth. Open my own eyes underwater and blink into the depths with bubbling cheeks. Beneath there lies the city, chewed in chocolate eruption, crystallized beneath a billion gallons. Perhaps in god's saliva, having drooled down in endless strings. Or perhaps his boohoo, stung, his translucent elbows and his knees, scabbed and wretched for our error, our soft days gobbling, furrowed, squeamed. Held breath burns. I am something. Way down, the billboards peel in blistered strips, shedding their color to the seahead. Face of a gone woman floating toward me, eyes as big as minivans. COCA COLA. ELECT FOR GOVERNOR. 1-800. WE BUY HOMES. Through the buildings' windows there are rooms. Within each room, filled up airtight—dust, carpet, lost hair, water cups, unopened mail, microscopics—the space in which small bodies negotiated, paddled, swore.

ON SWIMMING PAST OUR HOUSE

—Where Dad and I would wrestle. Where each night for a week before the raining my mom removed her brand new inset teeth, after a bird had smashed her first ones trying to fly straight down through her throat. Where in those last days I woke up choking on grasshoppers, the ceiling cracking. Water gushing from my ears. Snails in my breakfast. Sores in between my toes. I watched my father's face lose its pixels by the hour. My mother sweating blood and leaving spots on sofa pillows, the fridge, new patterns for our wallpaper. The cat having learned an awful language. Unlike others, I chose sleep. Passing now, I kick to swoop down deep enough to touch our roof, but each time I dive I make it only so far, an arm's length away before my lungs bunch and I must kick back numb and bubbling overhead.

RESURFACE

—Coming up I find again the water's face a rind. I bump and fumble with my back. The water wants me nearer, sucked into its gut. The mustache hairs on my top lip tremble. My brain goes Jell-o hot. I press and push, my blood babooning, until I birth a tunnel through the mud. My screaming lungs: a tulip blooming in fast-forward in reverse. Overhead the sky seems another surface, all reflection—as in, in the sky, I see the water. And there within it, me, muck-covered, huffing. I see myself seeing myself and we blink together, open-mouthed. I am older than I remember. I shaved my head once. I also had a child. We microwaved store milk in the bottle to make it warm. He'd coo and suck and sputter. I can feel him stretch inside me sometimes, reappeared back in there, unborn. Sometimes there is only color. I try to focus on my stroke: skull—slump—scissor—doggy paddle. My muscles ache in fever, sneezing. In want of something summered somewhere. I will go on until whenever.

BLOOM

—I will go on until the ocean spins and shoots its water in a funnel up to god. We here climb it—*we now? yes,* **we**—fast and fisting, scenting something overhead—*scorch of several summers? Wilting forests? Surely bleach.* When our tongues hang out they sizzle. A buzzing scums our eyes—*we who? who, we? my brothers, my baby, my, my, my sunning hum.*

More than a mile above, the earth is made of milk and foam. I see my mother in an outline made of pummel on the sea. Her rotten hair spindling up into me. Her goddamn hair. I can not breathe. I can not mumble. I climb higher into the thinning and turn around to look again. Her body shrunk into a compass, each node stirring soft spots in my mind—

N (at her temple)—*the rose thatch where, once young, I'd etched my chest, the marks still clear even now when observed in certain light;*

E (her tired left arm)—*that cross from church just downwind which they'd lifted off and painted black just before the sky invoked;*

S (around her bloated toes)—*Dad, his skin blood now, his blood skin, buried somewhere in the tide;*

W (her right hand's chubby fingers)—I could see nothing in this direction.

Somewhere below I hear the moan of those left over, rendered in tongues already half-forgotten or undone. I can recall the taste of years of toothpaste, our frozen dinners, the running rain, only when our sky height makes me vomit. *Come back down*, the them below us say. *We'll have you this time. We will breed.* I shake the echo off and look ahead, focused on the rhythm of my sizzling sweat to kill all and any other sound.

HOW THE BIRDS FLEW

—these newer birds, each made of metal, thorn and neon. They buzz around us by the hundred, snagging our skin in magnet. I can feel their nuzzle deep inside me, their squawk becoming logic, ways I know. Their shit drips down my white thighs with such weight I can barely further climb. I go dizzy. I see colors, hues no crayons had ever been. The others lost above me screaming. I swing my fists. I pop birds out of the air in rattle, their carcasses hailing into nowhere.

When I can breathe again, I climb on, my lungs humming with human dust. I hear the others, *yes, the others,* ahead of me up there, already grand. As I get higher it's cold enough to numb my head. Here the clouds hang thick in filament. The sun a gummy gunk and running. My sore skin peels. Under my skin, another something. With the voices gone and no others, I only briefly feel afraid.

OPERATIVE

—UP is on no compass. *DOWN* I'd have to learn to disregard.

FURTHER

—I slip a sheet of self under my tongue and taste tar. I can no longer see my mother. I climb to a clearing. She's still right there, her bloated body continental—eyes a hundred evenings wide—her voice—*Remember the sky that morning? The way it cracked up as an egg? The foam gushing out of everywhere: the gutters, the children's eye holes, the broken backbone of the sea?* Her rhythm pummels through me, moistening my brain with ugly dew. *Yes, come back down*, she snores into my stomach. The blood piddles and divides. *Come back and all will be well. We will learn.* Behind those oceanic eyes, though, such burn. Such unclear terror, laced with sting. I feel her weather. Fan her faint. I feel her finger in my knee. *My one, I swear, I promise, please...*

I turn and continue higher. I climb until the land is covered under curdle. Until I can't hear her singing and my head is full of pop. The air around me in a bonnet. The strum inside me strung with color. No nothing but a gleam.

I could wrap my arms around it—I could breathe it in—I did.

COMA OCEAN

— Some morning I will wake up. Come morning I'll wake up and. And the summer in my elbows. Sun at my elbows, stuttered open. Some morning I will stand up and the floor will swish beneath my feet. My new feet, bruised and washed white. White I wouldn't recognize, imagine. Imagine home. Some homecoming. I will move into those lost rooms, wet and depthless, and I will sit against the wall. I'll sit with the wall and watch the years unwrap a second span. My head. My lips unwrapped and chapped wide open. My colors spilling lather in the reek. Somewhere sandwiched solid something. Zeroes. Greased. Goodnight. Hello.

ACKNOWLEDGEMENTS

Thank you more than thanking to my parents, L.D. and Barbara, two unmatchables, without whom...

Thank you to my sister, Morgan, who knows, and to Justin.

Thank you to Heather for the time, and for our air.

Thank you to Zach and Jonathan for being, and believing.

Thank you to Michael Kimball, Keith Montesano, Ryan Call, for the wise eyes.

Thank you to Derek White, Robert Lopez, and Peter Markus, each a brother.

Thank you to Jesse Ball and Ken Sparling.

Thank you to Ken Baumann, Sean Kilpatrick, Mike Young, Sam Pink, Gene Morgan, Shane Jones, Jamie Iredell, Matthew Simmons, Lily Hoang, Chris Higgs, Justin Taylor, and Adam Robinson.

Thank you to a lot of other people also, whose names could fill another book.

ABOUT THE AUTHOR

Photo: Morgan Kendall

Blake Butler is the author of the novella EVER (Calamari Press). He edits 'the internet literature magazine blog of the future' HTML Giant, as well as two journals of innovative text: *Lamination Colony*, and concurrently with co-editor Ken Baumann, *No Colony*. His other writing has appeared in *The Believer*, *Unsaid*, *Fence*, Dzanc's *Best of the Web* 2009, as well as shortlisted in *Best American Nonrequired Reading* and widely online and in print. He lives in Atlanta, and blogs at gillesdeleuzecommittedsuicideandsowilldrphil.com.

FROM IN THE LIGHT I TOUCHED THE LIGHT   I KNEW THE LIGHT GREW

ER

A NOVELLA BY BLAKE BUTLER

CALAMARIPRESS.COM

ME | OR | OR WHAT | I COULD NOT THINK | I COULD NOT FIND THE WALL literature

NO COLONY DOT COM

NO COLONY DOT COM

featherproof BOOKSTORE

this is a CATALOG

featherproof books is an indie publisher based in Chicago, dedicated to the small-press ideals of finding fresh, urban voices. Our catalog features two categories of work: full-length, perfect-bound books like the one you hold in your hands, and downloadable mini-books available through **featherproof.com**. Our mini-books are individually designed short stories that can be downloaded for free and printed and assembled with ease. You can also order our books through our site at a friendly discount.

featherproof
light reading series

Life
Sentence
by Ambrose Austin

Max and
Emily
by Kate Axelrod

So Little
Impression
by Kyle Beachy

Marmal
is the
Sometimes
by Tobias Amadon
Bengelsdorf

Peanuts and
The Amazing
Gro-Beast
by Chris Bower

Every Night
is Bluegrass
Night
by Tobias Carroll

December
26th, 2004
by Brian Costello

Magic
by Mairead Case

Dear Michael
by Margaret Chapman

The Feast
of Saint
Eichatadt
by Pete Coco

Donovan's
Closet
by Elizabeth Crane

My Father's
Hands
by Mary Cross

Grandpa's
Brag Book
by Todd Dills

 All My
Homes
by Paul Fattaruso

 M is for
My Hair
by Abby Glowgower

 Shooting
Music
by Jeb Gleason-Allured

 Anniversary
by Laura Bramon Good

 Women/Girls
by Amelia Gray

 The Stork
by John Griswold

 Flash
Flicker Fire
by Mary Hamilton

 My Brother
by Lindsay Hunter

 Hospitable
Madness
by Jac Jemc

 This Is
by Andrea Johnson

 Witch of
the Bayou
by Rana Kelly

 Our
Pilgrimage
to Dollywood
by Heidi Laus

 By the
Rivers, We
Remember
by James Lower

 My Imaginary
Boyfriend
by Ling Ma

 101 Reasons
Not to Have
Children
by Ryan Markel

 Slave-
making
Ants
by Anne Elizabeth
Moore

 A Fourth of
July Party
by Kerri Mullen

 Saints
by Colleen O'Brien

 Sunday
Morning
by Susan Petrone

 In the Dream,
by Jay Ponteri

 Agee by the
Bedpost
by Caroline Picard

 Keftir the
Blind
by Nathaniel Rich

 The Camp
Psychic
by Kevin Sampsell

 And if I Kiss
You in the
Garden...
by Fred Sasaki

 The Lovers
of Vertigo
by Timothy Schaffert

 Flat Mindy
by Patrick Somerville

 The
Nightman
by Zach Stage

 Letter from
the Seaway
by Scott Stealey

 The
Diagnosis
of Sadness
by Jill Summers

the ENCHANTERS
vs.
Sprawlburg Springs

a novel by
Brian Costello

The Enchanters vs. Sprawlburg Springs is a satirical, riotous story of a band trapped in suburbia and bent on changing the world. A frenzied "scene" whips up around them as they gain popularity, and the band members begin thinking big. It's a hilarious, crazy send-up of self-destructive musicians written in a prose filled with more music than anything on the radio today.

SONS OF THE RAPTURE

a novel by
TODD DILLS

Billy Jones and his dad have a score to settle. Up in Chicago, Billy drowns his past in booze. In South Carolina, his father saddles up for a drive to reclaim him. Caught in this perfect storm is a ragged assortment of savants: shape-shifting doctor, despairingly bisexual bombshell, tiara-crowned trumpeter, zombie senator.

degrees of separation

Edited by Samia Saleem

Degrees of Separation features 33 detachable postcards from graphic designers with ties to New Orleans. Each one articulates their experiences and reflections upon Hurricane Katrina. This limited edition volume comes wrapped in a gorgeous customized sleeve.

HIDING OUT

decoys by jonathan messinger

Nothing is as it seems: A jilted lover dons robot armor to win back the heart of an ex-girlfriend; an angel loots the home of a single father; a teenager finds the key to everlasting life in a video game. In this much-anticipated debut, one of Chicago's most exciting young writers has crafted playful and empathic tales of misguided lonely hearts. Sparkling with humor and showcasing an array of styles, *Hiding Out* features characters dodging consequences while trying desperately to connect.

This Will Go Down on Your Permanent Record

by Susannah Felts

At the beginning of a lonely summer, 16-year-old Vaughn Vance meets Sophie Birch, and the two forge an instant and volatile alliance at Nashville's neglected Dragon Park. But when Vaughn takes up photography, she trains her lens on Sophie, and their bond dissolves as quickly as it came into focus. Felts keenly illuminates the pitfalls of coming of age as an artist, the slippery nature of identity, and the clash of class in the New South. *This Will Go Down on Your Permanent Record* is a sparkling and probing debut novel from a rising literary star.

boring boring boring boring boring boring boring

zachplague.com

When the mysterious gray book that drives their twisted relationship goes missing, Ollister and Adelaide lose their post-modern marbles. He plots revenge against art patriarch The Platypus, while she obsesses over their anti-love affair. Meanwhile, the art school set experiments with bad drugs, bad sex, and bad ideas. But none of these desperate young minds has counted on the intrusion of a punk named Punk and his potent sex drug. This wild slew of characters get caught up in the gravitational pull of The Platypus' giant art ball, where a confused art terrorism cell threatens a ludicrous and hilarious implosion. Zach Plague has written and designed a hybrid typo/graphic novel which skewers the art world, and those boring enough to fall into its traps. *boring boring boring boring boring boring boring* is an intrigue of mundane proportion.

a book by amelia gray

If anything's going to save the characters in Amelia Gray's debut from their troubled romances, their social improprieties, or their hands turning into claws, it's a John Mayer concert tee. In *AM/PM*, Gray's flash-fiction collection, impish humor is on full display. Tour through the lives of 23 characters across 120 stories full of lizard tails, Schrödinger boxes and volcano love. Follow June, who wakes up one morning covered in seeds; Leonard, who falls in love with a chaise lounge; and Andrew, who talks to his house in times of crisis. An intermittent love story as seen through a darkly comic lens, Gray mixes poetry and prose, humor and hubris to create a truly original piece of fiction.

GET HATCHED!

Sign up now for the new Paper Egg Books imprint from *f*eatherproof, and receive two limited-edition, subscription-only books in the mail (plus some other goodies). Each edition will feature one of our favorite up-and-coming authors, and will be designed by acclaimed artist and graphic novelist Paul Hornschemeier.

Check out: *papereggbooks.com*

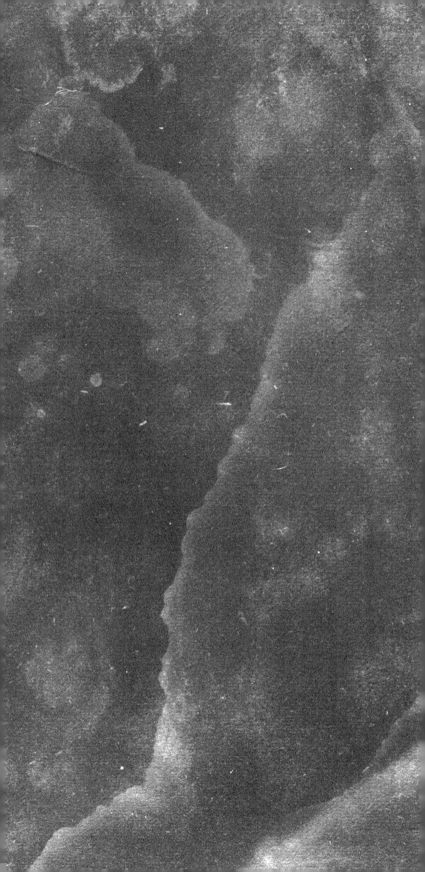

www.ingramcontent.com/pod-product-compliance
Lightning Source LLC
Jackson TN
JSHW011949131224
75386JS00042B/1634